NO AR

ISSUES THAT CONCERN YOU

Censorship

Ronald D. Lankford, Jr., *Book Editor*

GREENHAVEN PRESS
A part of Gale, Cengage Learning

GALE
CENGAGE Learning

Detroit • New York • San Francisco • New Haven, Conn • Waterville, Maine • London

Christine Nasso, *Publisher*
Elizabeth Des Chenes, *Managing Editor*

© 2010 Greenhaven Press, a part of Gale, Cengage Learning

Gale and Greenhaven Press are registered trademarks used herein under license.

For more information, contact:
Greenhaven Press
27500 Drake Rd.
Farmington Hills, MI 48331-3535
Or you can visit our Internet site at gale.cengage.com

ALL RIGHTS RESERVED.
No part of this work covered by the copyright herein may be reproduced, transmitted, stored, or used in any form or by any means graphic, electronic, or mechanical, including but not limited to photocopying, recording, scanning, digitizing, taping, Web distribution, information networks, or information storage and retrieval systems, except as permitted under Section 107 or 108 of the 1976 United States Copyright Act, without the prior written permission of the publisher.

For product information and technology assistance, contact us at

Gale Customer Support, 1-800-877-4253
For permission to use material from this text or product, submit all requests online at www.cengage.com/permissions

Further permissions questions can be e-mailed to permissionrequest@cengage.com

Articles in Greenhaven Press anthologies are often edited for length to meet page requirements. In addition, original titles of these works are changed to clearly present the main thesis and to explicitly indicate the author's opinion. Every effort is made to ensure that Greenhaven Press accurately reflects the original intent of the authors. Every effort has been made to trace the owners of copyrighted material.

Cover image copyright arenacreative, 2009. Used under license from Shutterstock.com.

LIBRARY OF CONGRESS CATALOGING-IN-PUBLICATION DATA

Censorship / Ronnie D. Lankford, book editor.
   p. cm. -- (Issues that concern you)
  Includes bibliographical references and index.
  ISBN 978-0-7377-4744-7
1. Censorship--United States--Juvenile literature. 2. Mass media--Censorship--Juvenile literature. 3. Internet--Censorship--Juvenile literature. I. Lankford, Ronald D., 1962-
  Z658.U5C393 2010
  363.310973--dc22
                                                    2009050038

Printed in the United States of America
1 2 3 4 5 6 7 14 13 12 11 10

CONTENTS

Censorship assumes many visible forms, from the banning of books in libraries and schools to the suppression of song lyrics on the radio and MTV. Movies were censored under the Hays Code in the United States for many years, and even today movies receive ratings that effectively limit who can see a particular movie by age. The Federal Communications Commission (FCC) continues to oversee the content of network television along with FM and AM radio and can effectively censor individually owned radio and television stations by refusing to renew licenses. In recent years a series of high-profile battles over censorship and the Internet have also occurred.

But censorship also assumes less obvious forms. It may be common knowledge, for instance, that public schools filter Internet content to prevent exposure to pornography, but less obvious censorship than filtering may sometimes block access to informational sites that include art and literary poetry. That school boards frequently ban controversial books from the classroom may be common knowledge, but that many librarians and teachers choose to not use books that may prove controversial is less obvious. Many social observers have also considered the regulations on student clothing and body art in public and private schools a form of censorship. Censorship, then, may occur in many ways.

Internet Censorship in Schools and Libraries

In 2001 the federal Children's Internet Protection Act (CIPA) was signed into law, and in 2003 the law was upheld by the Supreme Court. The law requires any public library or school that receives specific funds from the federal government to filter Internet searches. Twenty-one states also have written policies requiring public libraries and schools to filter Internet content. In general, these state and federal policies are attempting to limit

The widespread use of the Internet has raised new and troubling concerns regarding censorship and free speech.

access to pornography or any content considered harmful to minors (anyone under eighteen).

Critics, however, have noted that filtering Internet searches also limits access to many legitimate sites that may provide knowledge for young adults. These restrictions limit access to sites containing medical advice, birth control, and information on body image. A study in 2003 by the Electronic Frontier Foundation and Online Policy Group found that even with the most nonrestricting settings on commonly used filtering software, thousands of pages that would not be restricted under CIPA were blocked.

"Thus, certain content that is appropriate for minors under CIPA is blocked from their access," Eric J. Sinrod notes in *USA Today*. "Content relating to topics such as comedy, short poems, personal care and pogo-sticks was blocked by the software."[1]

Self-Censorship in Schools and Libraries

Multiple controversies surround books that have been chosen for middle and high school curricula, from John Steinbeck's *East of Eden* to J.K. Rowling's *Harry Potter and the Sorcerer's Stone*. But a number of books, observers have suggested, are never chosen for libraries or schools because of potential controversies. One example is Barry Lyga's *Boy Toy*, a young adult book that includes controversial sexual content. Bookstores that chose to carry the book, for example, placed *Boy Toy* in the adult section. The author of the book also heard a number of stories about librarians who loved the book, but who would not recommend buying it.

"It's sort of a soft, quiet, very insidious censorship, where nobody is raising a stink, nobody is complaining, nobody is burning books," Lyga told the *School Library Journal*. "They're just quietly making sure it doesn't get out there."[2]

One problem with understanding this form of censorship, however, is that it is very difficult to document. "It's probably fairly widespread," Pat Scales, the president of the Association of Library Services to Children, told the *School Library Journal*, "but we don't have any way of really knowing, because people who self-censor are not likely to broadcast it."[3]

School Censorship and Self-Expression

In recent years many schools have initiated strict dress code policies, including restrictions on tattoos and body piercings. Some of these changes occurred following a number of school shootings, where a link was drawn between style of clothing and the behavior of the attackers. Generally speaking, these codes have placed restrictions on clothing that reveals too much of a student's body, gang-related symbols, and any clothing item that suggests violence or promotes tobacco or alcohol use. Restrictions have also been placed on the length of boys' hair. In some instances, schools have even established student-uniform requirements.

These policies have posed two broad questions. One, whether these restrictions overly limit a student's freedom of expression; and two, who decides what will be restricted. In one case in Dearborn, Michigan, in 2003, a student was prohibited from wearing a T-shirt critical of President George W. Bush. The Michigan courts, however, later ruled that because the shirt had not caused a disturbance in the school (the student had worn the shirt for three hours before being asked to turn it inside out), he should be permitted to wear it. While civil libertarians interpreted this court decision as a victory for student rights, the federal and state courts have generally allowed school boards to set policy concerning clothing and body art.

Censorship as a Balancing Act

Many people wonder how the Internet or self-expression can be censored in countries like the United States that have amendments and laws that protect freedom of speech. In reality, however, these rights to freedom have often been balanced against many other concerns and beliefs. Perhaps the most obvious restriction concerning freedom of speech is that of age. Even while many forms of free expression have been sanctioned by the federal and state court system in the United States, it is still agreed upon that these forms are not always legally available to anyone under eighteen.

Few easy solutions or widely accepted compromises can be found when looking at the issue of censorship. Ideas about censorship evolve as new technologies like the Internet change how people access potentially controversial information. Within any culture, censorship is a constant balancing act between the legal precedents, public opinion, and everyday practices.

The issue of censorship in schools and libraries is one of the many topics that will be considered in this anthology. In articles taken from magazines, newspapers, Web sites, and Internet blogs, writers debate how a society balances individuals' right of free speech against broader social needs as defined by businesses, churches, and the government. In the appendix, the section titled "What You Should Know About Censorship" provides information for young people researching the issue; the section titled "What You Should Do About Censorship" offers information for young people who experience the issue of censorship. With all of these features, *Issues That Concern You: Censorship* provides an excellent resource for anyone interested in this timely issue.

Notes

1. Eric J. Sinrod, "CIPA-Regulated Filters Fall Short," *USA Today*, July 24, 2003. www.usatoday.com/tech/columnist/ericjsinrod/ 2003-07-22-sinrod_x.htm.
2. Debra Lau Whelan, "A Dirty Little Secret: Self-Censorship," *School Library Journal*, February 1, 2009. www.schoollibraryjour nal.com/article/CA6632974.html.
3. Whelan, "A Dirty Little Secret: Self-Censorship."

Parents Should Censor the Internet for Children

Amanda Paulson

Amanda Paulson is a staff writer for *The Christian Science Monitor*. In the following viewpoint, Paulson outlines the new guidelines from the Federal Trade Commission (FTC) about how to keep children and teens safe on the Internet. The FTC suggests that parents not react too harshly against technology by denying access to the Internet or using filters, but that they instead develop an ongoing conversation with their children about how to navigate the Internet safely. Kids and teens often have poor judgment and do not think about the potential ramifications of posting information about themselves online, and it is the job of their parents, and no one else, to guide them.

For parents who worried about the potential dangers in new technology, and are unsure how to help their kids navigate a wireless world safely, there may be comfort in the basic message from a new guide from the Federal Trade Commission (FTC): Talk to your kids.

Ultimately, simply addressing these issues with your kids—and emphasizing that the basic rules that guide communications offline are the same ones that should apply to communication

Amanda Paulson, "How to Keep Your Teen Safe on the Internet," *Christian Science Monitor*, December 16, 2009. Copyright © 2009 The Christian Science Publishing Society. All rights reserved. Reproduced by permission from Christian Science Monitor. www.csmonitor.com.

online—is what's important, says Nat Wood, an assistant director in the FTC's Bureau of Consumer Protection.

"The reach of modern communication technology means it can be really hard to step away from a mistake, but the principals of communicating in a civil way are the same online and off," says Mr. Wood, who worked on the FTC guide, known as Net Cetera. "In a lot of ways, this makes it easier on parents."

Still, the combination of typical teenage poor judgment with the far reach of today's technology haunts many parents, who

Concerned about the dangers of providing personal information on the Internet, many parents set up software parameters to control their children's online activities.

envision their teenagers being harassed by peers, stalked by a sexual predator, or answering questions from a potential boss or college admissions officer about the embarrassing photos they posted to their Facebook page.

Kids Need Parental Guidance

Valerie, a mother in North Dakota who prefers not to use her last name because of privacy concerns, was surprised when her 16-year-old daughter's cell phone started registering a lot of odd numbers. She went onto Michelle's MySpace page—available to anyone—and discovered she'd posted her number, and many other private details, along with the message, "I'm bored, text me."

"I think we fell down on the job by not being more cautious and watching more," says Valerie, who talked to Michelle and showed her how much personal data came up simply through googling her phone number. "She nearly had a heart attack," says Valerie. "It was a huge wake-up call when she saw how much was out there about her."

Michelle and her parents worked together to come up with some acceptable guidelines—don't share passwords, don't post questionable photos or sensitive information such as phone numbers or hometown, don't list your age.

Valerie and her husband also made a rule that the family laptop can't be taken into the kids' bedrooms.

That story is a fairly typical one, Internet-safety experts say: Kids don't mean to create problems, but often don't have the best judgment and don't think about the potential consequences.

But reacting too harshly—particularly by denying access to technology or using filters—is unlikely to work, and also denies the many positive aspects of new technology to increasingly-connected teenagers, they add.

"Teens whose parents are actively and positively involved in what their children are doing, both online and in the real world, are the ones who engage in less risky behavior online," says Nancy Willard, executive director of the Center for the Safe and Responsible Use of the Internet.

Parents Need to Talk Proactively to Kids

She also cautions parents against being too paranoid. The cyber-predator threat that was hyped in much of the past decade is exceedingly rare, she notes. The biggest dangers kids face online are from peers who misuse information or harass others, or from their own poor judgment in posting images that later reach the wrong people.

"The entire conversation with young people has to be focused on 'What are the potential harmful consequences?'" Ms. Willard says. "It's not rule-based, it's consequence-based."

Larry Rosen, a professor of psychology at California State University in Dominguez Hills and author of "Me, MySpace and I," agrees, and says that a lot of the issues today come from parents who are happy to let their kids be occupied by technology but never actively talk about it with them.

Talking to kids proactively—perhaps using a news story to raise the issue—is key, says Professor Rosen. "They don't have the best decision-making abilities, and they're just kids," he says.

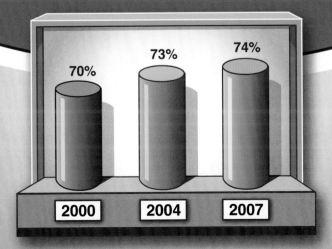

Home Computers Are Now Being Located in More Public Spaces

Parents are increasingly restricting kids to using a computer located in a public place within the home.

70%
73%
74%

2000
2004
2007

Taken from: Pew Internet and American Life Project, "Statistics," April 18, 2007.

Those approaches are also emphasized in the FTC guide, which provides a glossary of terms and explicit information about cyber-bullying, sexting, file sharing, and other potential sources of problems. The guide also points to the positive elements of kids' online communication and advises parents to start discussions [while their children are] young and keep communication channels open.

Net Cetera, the guide, "is value-neutral and caters neither to the 'left' nor the 'right,' but it encourages parents to communicate their own values to their kids," Jon Leibowitz, the FTC chairman, said [December 16, 2009] in releasing the guide. "When parents are up front about their values and how they apply in the online world, kids will make more thoughtful decisions when they face tricky situations."

TWO

The Government Should Censor the Internet for Children

Robert Peters

> Robert Peters is the president of Morality in Media, Inc. and believes that the Supreme Court's refusal to support legislation against online pornography has left children unprotected. The original lower court decision (that the Supreme Court supported by refusing to hear), Peters states, failed to take into account that children have more access to pornography online than they have had in the past. He believes the court was also shortsighted in not recognizing that, as children grow older, they often have Internet access outside of the home (at school, in libraries, and in the homes of friends). While the lower court may be responsible for not supporting antipornography legislation, it is the Supreme Court that has the ultimate responsibility, Peters suggests. He lists a number of previous cases in which the Supreme Court has undercut the strength of legislation designed to protect children from pornography. In the end, Peters believes, protecting children from pornography will require multiple methods, including government legislation.

Last Wednesday [January 21, 2009] the Supreme Court announced that it would not review a decision by the U.S. Court of Appeals in Philadelphia invalidating the Child Online

Robert Peters, "Protecting Children from Porn U.S. Supreme Court Says No," *Voice*, January 28, 2009. thevoicemagainze.com. Reproduced by permission of Morality in Media, Inc.

Protection Act [COPA]. COPA would have required websites that commercially distribute pornography to take reasonable steps to keep minors (defined as children under 17) away from the smut.

Thanks to the federal courts in Philadelphia and the U.S. Supreme Court, more than a decade has now passed since Congress first enacted laws to protect children from Internet pornography, and there are still no enforceable laws that require persons who commercially distribute pornography on the Internet to take reasonable steps to restrict children's access to that material.

Today, if a child were to walk into an "adult bookstore," he or she would be told to leave, because it is against the law to sell pornography to children in real space. But if that same child were to "click" to most commercial websites that distribute hardcore pornography, he or she could view pornography free of charge and without restriction, because when it comes to cyberspace, the federal courts think parental use of filters is an adequate solution to the problem.

Filtering and Monitoring Technology

Parental use of filtering and monitoring technology on computers under their control should be the "first line of defense" when it comes to protecting children from Internet pornography. But for any number of reasons, many parents will not use such technology. While it may come as a surprise to some federal judges, many parents are:

- Overburdened and exhausted
- Naive or too trusting
- Fearful of being too strict or of upsetting their children
- Concerned about filters blocking legitimate websites
- Technologically challenged or unable to afford technology
- Unable to speak or read English
- Physically or mentally disabled
- Abusive or neglectful of their children

In response to these concerns, the U.S. Court of Appeals in Philadelphia wrote:

The Government made much of a study that found that only 54% of parents use filters. . . . But the Government has neglected the fact that this figure represents a 65% increase from a prior study done four years earlier, which indicates that significantly more families are using filters. . . . Furthermore, the circumstance that some parents choose not to use filters does not mean that filters are not an effective alternative to COPA. Though we recognize that some of those parents may be indifferent to what their children see, others may have decided to use other methods to

Many feel that government should be actively involved in keeping children safe from Internet predators. National organizations like the Internet Keep Safe Coalition offer programs recommending that adults censor their children's Internet content.

protect their children—such as by placing the family computer in the living room . . . —or trust that their children will voluntarily avoid harmful material on the Internet.

Increased Exposure

Perhaps the Court of Appeals judges were ignorant of a study showing that while the percentage of parents who said they utilized filtering software did rise significantly in recent years, so did the percentages of children who said they were exposed to unwanted pornography or who said they went to an X-rated site on purpose.

Furthermore, according to the most recent survey that I am aware of [2007], only 41% of parents said that they "use parental controls to block their children's access to certain websites," despite the fact that for more than a decade government agencies (including schools), media outlets, online services, filter technology companies, and nonprofits have vigorously promoted parental use of filters.

And children in large numbers have been exposed to Internet pornography, as another recent [2008] study shows. "Overall, 72% of participants (93.2% of boys, 61.1% of girls) had seen online pornography before age 18. . . . Most exposure began when youth were ages 14 to 17, and boys were significantly more likely to view online pornography more often and to view more types of images."

Quite incredibly, the Court of Appeals judges ignored the reality that as children get older they can access the Internet outside the home (e.g., at a school, library, friend or relative's house or job). Increasingly, children can also access the Internet via mobile devices, and all it takes is one child in a group of friends to have unrestricted access to the Internet for all to have access.

Ignoring Previous Court Decisions

In turning a blind eye towards the fact that many parents do not use filters and that children can access the Internet on comput-

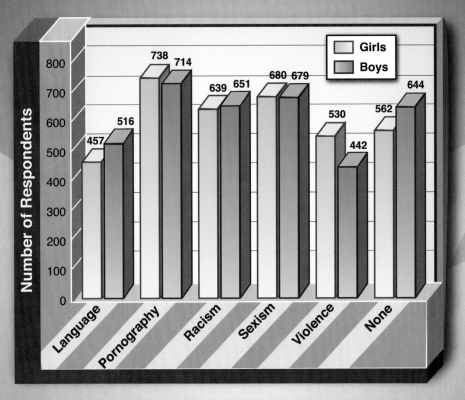

What Are Good Reasons to Censor Books, Magazines, and Other Media?

Taken from: Kids USA survey, "Censorship: Survey Results," http://teacher.scholastic.com.

ers that are not under parental control, these judges also ignored the Supreme Court's holding in *Ginsberg v. New York*, where the Court stated:

> While the supervision of children's reading may best be left to their parents, the knowledge that parental control or guidance cannot always be provided and society's transcendent interest in protecting the welfare of children justify reasonable regulation of the sale of material to them. It is, therefore, altogether fitting and proper for a state to include in a statute designed to regulate the

sale of pornography to children special standards, broader than those embodied in legislation aimed at controlling dissemination of such material to adults.

It is also clear from the Court of Appeals decision that the judges were more concerned about the burden that implementation of an age verification system would have on pornography distributors (financial costs) and potential users (anonymity concerns) than they were about the impact on children of exposure to pornography that depicts, among other things, "barely legal" teens, bestiality, bondage, flogging, gangbangs, "golden showers" (urine), group sex, incest, marital infidelity, prostitution, rape, "scat" (feces), torture, and unsafe sex galore.

The Court of Appeals judges were unwilling to construe the law to avoid perceived constitutional problems (e.g., to apply only to for-profit enterprises). "We normally do not strike down a statute on First Amendment grounds when a limiting instruction . . . could be placed on the challenged statute."

By determining that the "taken as a whole" requirement of the law is unconstitutionally vague, the Court of Appeals ignored the history of the "taken as a whole" concept, which was first introduced by Judge [Augustus] Hand of the U.S. Court of Appeals in Manhattan in the 1934 [*United States v. One Book Called*] *Ulysses* case and became part of the Supreme Court's "adult" obscenity definition in the 1966 *Memoirs* [*v. Massachusetts*] case. In the 1972 *Kois* [*v. Wisconsin*] case, the Supreme Court provided guidance as to how the "taken [as] a whole" requirement could be applied to mediums other than a book or film. The Philadelphia judges also ignored the recent [*United States v.*] *Williams* case, which stated "perfect clarity and precise guidance have never been required even of regulations that restrict expressive activity."

Much more could be said about the COPA litigation in Philadelphia, including the judges' handling of the foreign-based website problem and the facts that COPA would not have applied to all Internet "modalities" and that age verification technology isn't perfect. Suffice it to say for purposes of these comments, in my opinion it is no coincidence that pornography defenders have in recent years chosen the Third Circuit to challenge four different federal laws intended to protect children from smut. Third Circuit judges determined that all four were unconstitutional.

The Supreme Court and Pornography

In fairness to the Philadelphia judges, however, the buck must stop at the U.S. Supreme Court.

The Supreme Court's penchant for striking down laws intended to protect children from speech that is harmful to children and unprotected by the First Amendment for children began in earnest in the 1997 *Reno v. ACLU* [American Civil Liberties Union] case, where the Court invalidated a law intended to restrict children's access to "indecent" content disseminated on the Internet. In retrospect, I think Congress was unwise to attempt to regulate indecency on the entire Internet, but the Supreme Court was also unwise in assuming that parental use of filters would protect children from Internal smut.

In *Reno*, the Court was willing to put its trust in filters even before there was clear proof that they would be effective ("the evidence indicates that 'a reasonably effective method by which parents can prevent their children from accessing sexually explicit and other material which parents may believe is inappropriate for their children will soon be available.'").

But the deathblow to children's wellbeing came in the 2000 *U.S. v. Playboy* case, where the Supreme Court invalidated a needed and reasonable law that would have required cable TV operators to completely scramble signals for pay pornography channels, so that the signals would not bleed into homes of non-subscribers, or wait until 10 P.M. before airing the smut.

In applying "strict scrutiny" to this law, the *Playboy* Court ignored prior case law and in effect held that with the exception of broadcast TV, it is OK to expose children to pornography as long as parents have a means to plug up the smut, either before or after their children's exposure, even if many don't use that means for one reason or another, including failure to discover the problem.

In applying "strict scrutiny" to a law intended to restrict children's access to harmful content that is not constitutionally protected for children, because the law incidentally burdened adult access to that content, the *Playboy* Court did for the protection of children from pornography what the *Memoirs* Court did for the protection of society from obscene materials in 1966. It brought protection to an end, for as the Court said in the *Playboy* case, "it is rare that a regulation restricting speech because of its content will ever be permissible."

In the COPA litigation, the Supreme Court again applied "strict scrutiny" to a law intended to restrict children's access to content that is harmful to children and that is not protected speech for children, because that law incidentally burdened adult access to the content.

Restricting Pornography Requires Multiple Methods

The Court's COPA analysis would have made sense if the Government had a choice between two means, each of which could achieve the legitimate purpose of protecting children from Internet smut, one of which was less restrictive of First Amendment rights than the other. But the reality is that there is no one solution to protecting children from Internet smut, and just about everyone seems to understand that, except for ACLU lawyers and their expert witnesses and federal court judges in Philadelphia and Washington, DC.

Some societal problems do not permit any feasible either-or choice to achieve the governmental purpose. For example, to protect children from online sexual exploitation, parental involvement, technology, schools, nonprofit organizations, and laws are all needed. Now, Internet service providers, credit card companies, and banks are also cooperating with this effort.

And to protect children from Internet pornography, parents, technology, schools, nonprofit organizations, online services and laws will also be necessary. By invalidating reasonable and necessary laws intended to protect children from Internet pornography, the Court has turned a deaf ear to the warning enunciated in *Columbia Broadcasting System v. Democratic National Committee*:

> In evaluating the First Amendment claims . . . we must afford great weight to the decisions of Congress. . . . Professor Chafee aptly observed: "Once we get away from the bare words of the Amendment, we must construe it as part of a Constitution which creates a government for the purpose of performing several very important tasks. The Amendment should be interpreted so as to not cripple the regular work of government."

Our nation's founding fathers viewed the First Amendment within a framework of ordered liberty, not as a license to sell smut without any legal obligation to restrict children's access. In the COPA litigation, the Supreme Court has done this nation a disservice.

THREE

Talk Radio Should Be Censored

John Halpin, James Heidbreder, Mark Lloyd, Paul Woodhull, Ben Scott, Josh Silver, and S. Derek Turner

John Halpin, James Heidbreder, Mark Lloyd, Paul Woodhull, Ben Scott, Josh Silver, and S. Derek Turner are members of the Center for American Progress, a think tank that works toward improving the lives of Americans through ideas and action. In 2007 the group, along with Free Press, authored a joint report on what they viewed as an imbalance relating to political talk radio. The following report finds that even though a wide variety of media sources is available for consumers today, most Americans continue to listen to the radio as much as nineteen hours per week. The report's authors, however, believe that radio's news and talk shows are imbalanced, with conservative sources dominating the programming. For instance, on any given weekday, the authors note, conservative talk stations account for 2,570 hours and 15 minutes of programming compared to 254 hours for progressive talk radio. This raises the question, the authors of the study insist, that talk radio may not be fully representing all Americans. The authors believe that this imbalance has been created by structural problems in the federal regulation of radio, including the elimination of the Fairness Doctrine (which generally stated that equal

John Halpin, James Heidbreder, Mark Lloyd, Paul Woodhull, Ben Scott, Josh Silver, and S. Derek Turner, "The Structural Imbalance of Political Talk Radio," Center for American Progress and Free Press, June 21, 2007. Reproduced by permission.

air time would be provided for controversial subjects). The authors of the report suggest that a number of regulations need to be reinstated to guarantee that radio is meeting the needs of local populations.

Despite the dramatic expansion of viewing and listening options for consumers today, traditional radio remains one of the most widely used media formats in America. Arbitron, the national radio ratings company, reports that more than 90 percent of Americans ages 12 or older listen to radio each week, "a higher penetration than television, magazines, newspapers, or the Internet." Although listening hours have declined slightly in recent years, Americans listened on average to 19 hours of radio per week in 2006.

Among radio formats, the combined news/talk format (which includes news/talk/information and talk/personality) leads all others in terms of the total number of stations per format and trails only country music in terms of national audience share. Through more than 1,700 stations across the nation, the combined news/talk format is estimated to reach more than 50 million listeners each week.

As this report will document in detail, conservative talk radio undeniably dominates the format:

- Our analysis in the spring of 2007 of the 257 news/talk stations owned by the top five commercial station owners reveals that 91 percent of the total weekday talk radio programming is conservative, and 9 percent is progressive.
- Each weekday, 2,570 hours and 15 minutes of conservative talk are broadcast on these stations compared to 254 hours of progressive talk—10 times as much conservative talk as progressive talk.
- A separate analysis of all of the news/talk stations in the top 10 radio markets reveals that 76 percent of the programming in these markets is conservative and 24 percent is progressive, although programming is more balanced in markets such as New York and Chicago.

Talk Radio: Political Programming, May 2007

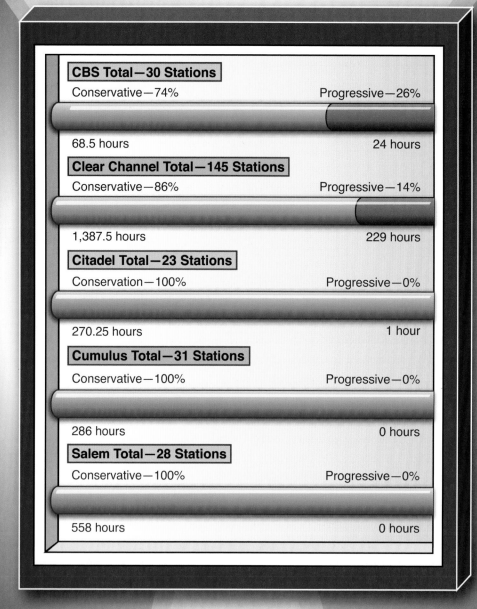

CBS Total—30 Stations

Conservative—74%   Progressive—26%

68.5 hours   24 hours

Clear Channel Total—145 Stations

Conservative—86%   Progressive—14%

1,387.5 hours   229 hours

Citadel Total—23 Stations

Conservation—100%   Progressive—0%

270.25 hours   1 hour

Cumulus Total—31 Stations

Conservative—100%   Progressive—0%

286 hours   0 hours

Salem Total—28 Stations

Conservative—100%   Progressive—0%

558 hours   0 hours

Taken from: Center for American Progress, "The Structural Imbalance of Political Talk Radio," June 21, 2007.

This dynamic is repeated over and over again no matter how the data is analyzed, whether one looks at the number of stations, number of hours, power of stations, or the number of programs. While progressive talk is making inroads on commercial stations, conservative talk continues to be pushed out over the airwaves in greater multiples of hours than progressive talk is broadcast.

These empirical findings may not be surprising given general impressions about the format, but they are stark and raise serious questions about whether the companies licensed to broadcast over the public airwaves are serving the listening needs of all Americans.

There are many potential explanations for why this gap exists. The two most frequently cited reasons are the repeal of the Fairness Doctrine in 1987 and simple consumer demand. As this report will detail, neither of these reasons adequately explains why conservative talk radio dominates the airwaves.

Our conclusion is that the gap between conservative and progressive talk radio is the result of multiple structural problems in the U.S. regulatory system, particularly the complete breakdown of the public trustee concept of broadcast, the elimination of clear public interest requirements for broadcasting, and the relaxation of ownership rules including the requirement of local participation in management.

Ownership diversity is perhaps the single most important variable contributing to the structural imbalance based on the data. Quantitative analysis conducted by Free Press of all 10,506 licensed commercial radio stations reveals that stations owned by women, minorities, or local owners are statistically less likely to air conservative hosts or shows.

In contrast, stations controlled by group owners—those with stations in multiple markets or more than three stations in a single market—were statistically more likely to air conservative talk. Furthermore, markets that aired both conservative and progressive programming were statistically less concentrated than the markets that aired only one type of programming and were more likely to be the markets that had female- and minority-owned stations.

The radio talk show of conservative host Rush Limbaugh (pictured) has nine times the number of listeners as his closest progressive competitor.

The disparities between conservative and progressive programming reflect the absence of localism in American radio markets. This shortfall results from the consolidation of ownership in radio stations and the corresponding dominance of syndicated programming operating in economies of scale that do not match the local needs of all communities.

This analysis suggests that any effort to encourage more responsive and balanced radio programming will first require steps to increase localism and diversify radio station ownership to better meet local and community needs. We suggest three ways to accomplish this:

- Restore local and national caps on the ownership of commercial radio stations.
- Ensure greater local accountability over radio licensing.
- Require commercial owners who fail to abide by enforceable public interest obligations to pay a fee to support public broadcasting.

FOUR

Talk Radio Should Not Be Censored

Brian Jennings, interviewed by Al Peterson

In an interview with journalist Al Peterson, author Brian Jennings talks about his book *Censorship: The Threat to Silence Talk Radio*. One of Jennings' main concerns is the possible revival of the Fairness Doctrine, a previous Federal Communications Commission (FCC) policy that required radio stations to offer equal coverage on controversial issues. By reviving the doctrine, he believes, the government will be regulating content on the airwaves. Jennings asserts that this strategy has a specific aim: to halt the success of conservative talk radio programs. Nonetheless, he says that the revival of the Fairness Doctrine is neither a conservative nor a liberal issue and that both sides should band together to protect freedom of speech.

Talk radio veteran Brian Jennings, most recently VP of News/Talk/Sports programming for Citadel Broadcasting, is just about to release his highly anticipated book on how a return of the Fairness Doctrine will impact Talk radio and free speech in America. *Censorship: The Threat to Silence Talk Radio* is a call to arms to all Americans—liberal and conservative, Republican and Democrat—to stand up for freedom of speech and to stand united against government regulation of content on

NTS Media Online, "Censorship's Threat to Talk Radio," April 24, 2009. Reproduced by permission.

the air. On the eve of his new book's publication (it [would arrive] in stores May 5, 2009) I spoke with Jennings to learn just why he's so passionate about his cause and why he says you can't trust what some politicians say vs. what they really plan to do with regard to this issue in the weeks and months ahead.

Al Peterson: *What inspired you to write the book?*

Brian Jennings: About two or three years ago I was driving between Atlanta and Charleston, SC listening to [Dial-Global syndicated talker] Neal Boortz. He did an hour or two on the whole issue of the Fairness Doctrine [requiring stations to cover both sides of a controversial issue] that day and he pointed out how

Many conservative talk show hosts, like the host pictured here, are concerned about the government's possible revival of the Fairness Doctrine, fearing that it will infringe on free speech.

Democrats in Congress were beginning to lineup to begin a push to regulate content on radio. My first reaction was, "that's ridiculous, that'll never happen." But the more I listened and the more I thought about it, the more I thought he was on to something. I'd say that was probably what first inspired me to begin focusing on writing the book.

Peterson: *Why should conservative Talk radio be afraid of the idea of presenting fair and balanced programming?*

Jennings: I don't think conservative Talk radio is afraid of that at all. In fact, I think that conservative Talk radio often does present both sides of an issue, whether it's in the host's monologue, or from callers who are always there to present the other side. My problem is with the government getting into the business of regulating content. Government has no business in regulating content, thought, or free speech in America. The marketplace should determine what it wants and doesn't want to hear. When government gets into the content regulation business we no longer have free speech and the First Amendment becomes meaningless at that point. I can't say it strongly enough; government has no business regulating content.

Peterson: *But doesn't the government already regulate content? How about those infamous words you can't say on broadcast radio and TV?*

Jennings: That is, in fact, content regulation. Frankly, I'm not for that either. I believe that the marketplace and common sense should determine how we view language in America. I would never use those words if I were behind a microphone, and I think most broadcasters would not use them, either. Sure, one will slip through now and then, but as a rule most broadcasters act responsibly. Again, when government sets a precedent of regulating content on radio, where does it stop? I believe that if we allow the government to regulate content, we become a society that is quickly headed toward tyranny—something I think we're already in the first stages of, to be honest with you.

Peterson: *President Obama and other Congressional leaders have stated they don't support a return of the Fairness Doctrine, so why should broadcasters worry?*

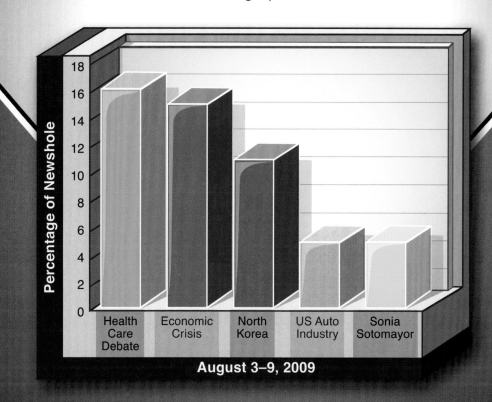

Health Care Coverage Tops Diverse News Agenda

The "newshole" is the space that must be filled by news content on television and radio. The data below show that health care dominated the newshole during a particular week in 2009.

Percentage of Newshole

August 3–9, 2009

Taken from: Michael Calderone, "Health Care Dominated Cable, Radio," August 11, 2009. www.politico.com.

Jennings: Because they're lying. They *do* want a Fairness Doctrine, but they realize they won't get one under that name because there'd be such a groundswell against it across America. But make no mistake of their intent to get it, through stealth initiatives and backdoor tactics that will accomplish their goal without having to take the heat from the American public. [U.S. Senate Leader] Harry Reid (D-NV) says he doesn't support a return to the Doctrine, while knowing full well that he already has Senator Richard Durbin's (D-IL) language in a bill that will allow the FCC [Federal Communications Commission] to do exactly what the Democratic party platform called for in 2008: more "diversity" and "localism." What those words really mean is the breaking up of media companies to force more liberalism into the conservative Talk radio landscape. I find it to be absolutely hypocritical.

Peterson: *It wouldn't actually take legislation to reinstate the Fairness Doctrine, would it?*

Jennings: No. In fact, Congress will probably sidestep the issue so that they won't have to take credit, or criticism for it. They'll use the FCC to get into so-called diversity issues with the idea that they can break down large media conglomerates and create more minority ownership, hoping that will lead to more diverse programming—that's the real goal. The other thing that concerns me is the proposals for mandated "advisory boards." We already have them. They're called "listeners" and "advertisers." They tell broadcasters everyday what's working and what isn't. Advisory boards don't need to be mandated.

Peterson: *How do you respond to critics who will say this is just another book written for the vast right wing conspiracy?*

Jennings: That's OK with me. Let them say whatever they want. I think we are in danger of losing our free speech rights in this country. I've dealt with this issue and worked with it since the early 1980s. Nobody has to convince me that this issue is real, because I've been there on the front lines, fighting it for decades. I spent half my career in radio under the Fairness Doctrine and the other half without it, so I do understand the difference. This should not be a fight of conservatives against liberals, or liberals against conservatives. It should be a fight of conservatives and liberals joined together in a fight against government regulation of free speech rights.

FIVE

The U.S. Military Censors Movies

David L. Robb

> David L. Robb is a journalist who has been nominated for the Pulitzer Prize three times. In his book *Operation Hollywood* he argues that the U.S. military strives to censor and shape material that it considers vital to its image. Robb notes that no one—neither the military nor Hollywood—wishes to admit this secret publicly. Because Hollywood can save millions of dollars by using Pentagon equipment, he maintains, it has been willing to submit to military censorship; for those directors and producers unwilling to cooperate, the military simply refuses to offer help. This relationship creates a fundamental conflict within American democracies, Robb believes, because the military —which is a government institution—is using its power to create propaganda. The only way that the military can be brought back into line, he believes, is for Congress to hold the Pentagon responsible for its breaches against the First Amendment pertaining to freedom of speech.

We may think that the content of American movies is free from government interference, but in fact, the Pentagon has been telling filmmakers what to say—and what not to say— for decades. It's Hollywood's dirtiest little secret.

David L. Robb, *Operation Hollywood: How the Pentagon Shapes and Censors Movies.* Amherst, NY: Prometheus, 2004. Copyright © 2004 by David L. Robb. Reproduced by permission.

Film and TV producers have allowed this to happen because collaborating with the Pentagon can save them a lot of money. Millions of dollars can be shaved off a film's budget if the military agrees to lend its equipment and assistance. And all a producer has to do to get that assistance is submit five copies of the script to the Pentagon for approval; make whatever script changes the Pentagon suggests; film the script exactly as approved by the Pentagon; and prescreen the finished product for Pentagon officials before it's shown to the public.

It's a devil's bargain that's a good deal for both sides. And the only thing Hollywood likes more than a good movie is a good deal.

"They make prostitutes of us all because they want us to sell out to their point of view," says filmmaker Oliver Stone, who was refused military assistance for his Vietnam War–era films *Platoon* and *Born on the Fourth of July.*

"They want a certain kind of movie made," Stone says. "They don't want to deal with the downside of war. They assist movies that don't tell the truth about combat, and they don't assist movies that seek to tell the truth about combat. Most films about the military are recruiting posters."

This collaboration works because the Pentagon has what Hollywood wants—access to billions of dollars worth of sophisticated military hardware to put into movies; and Hollywood has what the Pentagon wants—access to the eyeballs of millions of viewers and potential recruits. And the Pentagon is quite candid about why it provides this assistance to Hollywood. According to the army's own handbook, A *Producer's Guide to U.S. Army Cooperation with the Entertainment Industry*, this collaboration must "aid in the recruiting and retention of personnel." . . .

Controlling the Arts

[But] no society is free that allows its military to control the arts. In America, it is not only unconscionable, it is unconstitutional. Allowing the world's most powerful military to place propaganda into the world's most powerful medium—unchecked and

For two of his films, Born on the Fourth of July *and* Platoon, *director Oliver Stone (pictured) declined assistance from the military, believing that the Pentagon uses moviemakers to promote its own agenda.*

unregulated—for over fifty years has certainly helped the Pentagon get more recruits for the armed forces and ever-increasing appropriations from Congress, but what is its long-term effect on the psyche of the American people?

In North Korea, the people are required to have speaker boxes in their homes that they can't turn off and that constantly pipe in propaganda. In America, we can turn off our television sets, but the military propaganda that is inserted into our television programs in the form of films and TV shows is done so subtly that the American people don't even know it's there.

Propaganda is used in North Korea to make the people there more accustomed to being constantly on a war footing. But might this not be an unintended consequence in the United States as well of allowing the Pentagon to shape, sanitize, and censor American films and television programs? Certainly, the American people have become a more warlike people in the last fifty years.

In 1940, the American people refused to go to war against Nazi Germany and Imperial Japan even as they overran Europe and Asia. Pres. Franklin Roosevelt knew then that the American people would not support a war unless the United States was attacked first.

But today the American people seem willing to go to war at the drop of a hat.

In the 1960s, the Vietnam War was launched on the flimsiest of pretexts: That North Vietnamese gunboats had allegedly attacked U.S. warships—a charge we now know to be false. In the 1980s, Libya was bombed by American jet fighters because a suspected Libyan terrorist had blown up a discothèque in Germany. In the 1990s, the United States attacked Iraq because it invaded Kuwait. And in 2003, the United States attacked Iraq again because Pres. George W. Bush said it was harboring weapons of mass destruction—weapons that were never found. And most Americans supported these wars.

And now Bush says that the United States has abandoned its decades-long policy of never using nuclear weapons in a first-strike attack. And the American people seem to support this, as well.

A Warrior Society

Is it possible that being saturated with military propaganda in films and TV shows over the last fifty years has made us a more warlike people? Is it possible that it could have had no effect?

The stakes are too high for these questions to remain unanswered, let alone unasked. The very character of the American people may be at stake.

The Pentagon has bribed, coerced, and intimidated filmmakers long enough. For too long, Hollywood has cravenly caved in to the Pentagon's demands to change its stories to make the military look good. It is time to put an end to the disgraceful relationship between Hollywood and the Pentagon.

Congress should act. It has neglected its oversight responsibilities long enough. Congress, which is supposed to keep an eye on the way the Pentagon is spending the taxpayers' money, has only asked the Pentagon to explain its relationship with Hollywood twice—once in 1956 and again in 1969—and both times the Pentagon lied.

Congress should launch its first full and complete investigation into the Pentagon's role in the filmmaking process. Congress funds the Pentagon's activities, and Congress should stop it. The First Amendment to the Constitution states that "Congress shall make no law . . . abridging the freedom of speech. . . ." But by approving appropriation bills that fund the Pentagon's film office, Congress has done just that.

The Writers Guild of America [WGA] should act. The WGA, which claims to protect the creative rights of its members, has never once complained about the Pentagon altering its members' scripts. It has been silent long enough. The WGA should go on record opposing this blatant form of censorship, and it should insist in its next round of contract negotiations that companies that sign the WGA's contract will no longer be allowed to show a writer's script to anyone outside the company. This would effectively stop the Pentagon from ever looking at another writer's script.

Taking Action

The American public should also take action. They should write angry letters to Congress demanding an investigation. And a class-action lawsuit should be filed on behalf of all moviegoers [to seek] a court-ordered injunction to stop the Pentagon from tampering with the First Amendment rights of screenwriters, and to protect the public from being bombarded with military recruiting propaganda being placed in films without the public's knowledge. The public should also boycott any film—whether shown in theaters or on home video or DVD—that has been made with the cooperation of the military. If an informed and outraged public takes the economic incentive out of such collaborations, the practice will stop immediately.

Even without Pentagon subsidies, Hollywood will still turn out plenty of movies and TV shows about the military. That's because of one simple fact: Hollywood loves heroes, and the military has more of them than anyone else. Hollywood doesn't need police department subsidies to turn out movies about hero cops. It doesn't need subsidies from the American Medical Association to produce shows about heroic doctors. It doesn't need fire department subsidies to turn out TV shows about heroic firemen.

Hollywood will still want access to the military's tanks, jets, submarines, and aircraft carriers, and the Pentagon will still be able to show off its hardware—and turn a profit—by making it available to bona fide producers under a schedule of uniform fees. It would cost producers more money, but in the end, it will be cheaper than scrapping the First Amendment.

SIX

Hollywood Self-Censors Movies

John Pilger

Journalist John Pilger believes that people have little need to worry about government censorship of war movies: In truth, Hollywood has a history of self-censorship. Beginning in the late 1970s, he notes, Hollywood covered the Vietnam War as an American tragedy, ignoring the millions of Vietnamese killed in the conflict. Unfortunately, Pilger maintains, even movie critics have failed to point out the underlying politics of Hollywood censorship. When movies attempt to tackle these difficult issues, he argues, it is difficult to get distribution in countries like the United States. Even in perilous times with multiple military conflicts around the world, Hollywood remains focused on "introspective dross" and escapist entertainment, Pilger says. He believes new, hard-hitting movies are needed to explore these current crises.

When I returned from the war in Vietnam, I wrote a film script as an antidote to the myth that the war had been an ill-fated noble cause. The producer David Puttnam took the draft to Hollywood and offered it to the major studios, whose responses were favorable—well, almost. Each issued a report card

John Pilger, "Hollywood's New Censors," *New Statesman*, February 19, 2009. Reproduced by permission of the author.

in which the final category, "politics," included comments such as: "This is real, but are the American people ready for it? Maybe they'll never be."

By the late 1970s, Hollywood judged Americans ready for a different kind of Vietnam movie. The first was *The Deer Hunter* which, according to *Time*, "articulates the new patriotism." The film celebrated immigrant America, with [actor] Robert de Niro as a working class hero ("liberal by instinct") and the Vietnamese as sub-human Oriental barbarians and idiots, or "gooks." The dramatic peak was reached during recurring orgiastic scenes in which GIs [U.S. soldiers] were forced to play Russian roulette by their Vietnamese captors. This was made up by the director Michael Cimino, who also made up a story that he had served in Vietnam. "I have this insane feeling that I was there," he said. "Somehow . . . the line between reality and fiction has become blurred."

Revising American History

The Deer Hunter was regarded virtually as documentary by ecstatic critics. "The film that could purge a nation's guilt!" said the *Daily Mail*. President Jimmy Carter was reportedly moved by its "genuine American message." Catharsis [emotional cleansing] was at hand. The Vietnam movies became a revisionist popular history of the great crime in Indo-China. That more than four million people had died terribly and unnecessarily and their homeland poisoned to a wasteland was not the concern of these films. Rather, Vietnam was an "American tragedy," in which the invader was to be pitied in a blend of false bravado-and-angst: sometimes crude (the *Rambo* films) and sometimes subtle ([director] Oliver Stone's *Platoon*). What mattered was the strength of the purgative.

None of this, of course, was new; it was how Hollywood created the myth of the Wild West, which was harmless enough unless you happened to be a Native American; and how the Second World War has been relentlessly glorified, which may be harmless enough unless you happen to be one of countless innocent human beings, from Serbia to Iraq, whose deaths or dispossession are justified by moralizing references to 1939–45. Hollywood's gooks, its *Untermenschen* [Nazi term for inferior people], are essential to this crusade—the dispatched Somalis in [director] Ridley Scott's *Black Hawk Down* and the sinister Arabs in movies like *Rendition*, in which the torturing CIA is absolved by [actor] Jake Gyllenhaal's good egg. As [journalists] Robbie Graham and Mark Alford pointed out in their *New Statesman* enquiry into corporate control of the cinema (2 February [2009]), in 167 minutes of [director] Steven Spielberg's *Munich*, the Palestinian cause is restricted to just two and a half minutes. "Far from being an 'even-handed cry for peace', as one critic claimed," they wrote, "*Munich* is more easily interpreted as a corporate-backed endorsement of Israeli policy."

Burying the Truth

With honorable exceptions, film critics rarely question this and identify the true power behind the screen. Obsessed with celebrity actors and vacuous narratives, they are the cinema's lobby correspondents, its dutiful press corps. Emitting safe snipes and sneers, they promote a deeply political system that dominates most of what we pay to see, knowing not what we are denied. [Director] Brian de Palma's 2007 film *Redacted* shows an Iraq the media does not report. He depicts the homicides and gang-rapes that are never prosecuted and are the essence of any colonial conquest. In the New York *Village Voice*, the critic Anthony Kaufman, in abusing the "divisive" De Palma for his "perverse tales of voyeurism and violence," did his best to taint the film as a kind of heresy and to bury it.

In this way, the "war on terror"—the conquest and subversion of resource rich regions of the world, whose ramifications and oppressions touch all our lives—is almost excluded from the popular cinema. [Director] Michael Moore's outstanding *Fahrenheit 911* was a freak; the notoriety of its distribution ban by the Walt Disney Company helped to force its way into cinemas. My own 2007 film *The War on Democracy*, which inverted the "war

Director Brian de Palma's (pictured) 2007 film about the Iraq war, Redacted, was criticized by one critic for depicting "perverse tales of voyeurism and violence."

on terror" in Latin America, was distributed in Britain, Australia and other countries but not in the United States. "You will need to make structural and political changes," said a major New York distributor. "Maybe get a star like [actor] Sean Penn to host it—he likes liberal causes—and tame those anti-[George W.] Bush sequences."

During the cold war, Hollywood's state propaganda was unabashed. The classic 1957 dance movie, *Silk Stockings*, was an anti-Soviet diatribe interrupted by the fabulous footwork of Cyd Charisse and Fred Astaire. These days, there are two types of censorship. The first is censorship by introspective dross. Betraying its long tradition of producing gems, escapist Hollywood is consumed by the corporate formula: just make 'em long and asinine and hope the hype will pay off. [English comedian] Ricky Gervais is his clever comic self in *Ghost Town*, while around him stale, formulaic characters sentimentalize the humor to death.

These are extraordinary times. Vicious colonial wars and political, economic and environmental corruption cry out for a place on the big screen. Yet, try to name one recent film that has dealt with these, honestly and powerfully, let alone satirically. Censorship by omission is virulent. We need another *Wall Street*, another *Last Hurrah*, another *Dr. Strangelove*. The partisans who tunnel out of their prison in Gaza, bringing in food, clothes, medicines and weapons with which to defend themselves, are no less heroic than the celluloid-honored POWs [prisoners of war] and partisans of the 1940s. They and the rest of us deserve the respect of the greatest popular medium.

SEVEN

Internet Providers Should Not Aid Government Censors

Rebecca MacKinnon

Rebecca MacKinnon is a journalist who has covered China for CNN. MacKinnon believes that American Internet companies like Google and Yahoo are aiding the Chinese government by offering censored search engines to the Chinese public. While the U.S. Congress has suggested a bill that would stop the practice of using a censored version of these search engines, she notes, the bill would also give the U.S. government excessive power to oversee Internet providers. While many Internet users in China are glad that Yahoo and Google remain available, she explains, many are angry at Internet providers who have turned over privacy information to the Chinese government. MacKinnon states that the congressional bill is a good place to start a conversation about Internet censorship in other countries, but that much more work will need to be done.

B ack in the late 1990s, when I was working as a journalist in China, I happened to read [author] Timothy Garton Ash's *The File*. It's a personal account about what happened in East Germany soon after the Berlin wall fell, when East Germans were suddenly able to access their Stasi [Ministry for State Security] police files. As it turned out, secret police informants in-

Rebecca MacKinnon, "America's Online Censors," *Nation*, February 24, 2006. Copyright © 2006 by The Nation Magazine/The Nation Company, Inc. Reproduced by permission.

cluded neighbors, lovers, spouses and in some cases even people's own children. One evening over dinner with some Chinese friends, I described the book and asked how they thought things might play out in a post-Communist China. One friend replied: "That day will come in China too. Then I'll know who my real friends are." The table fell silent.

Today China's leaders are fighting hard not to follow their East German and Soviet counterparts into the dustbin of history. Newspaper and magazine editors who have dared to publish stories exposing government lies and abuses of power have recently been sacked. Behind-the-scenes accounts of the sackings, defiant statements by the sacked editors and reproductions of the offending articles have spread like viruses all over the Chinese Internet. Chinese censors, enlisting the help of private Internet companies —both domestic and foreign—have been working overtime to remove the offending content. But they simply can't keep up with the viral spread of information in cyberspace.

The question is not whether the Chinese Communist Party will succeed in hanging on to power. The real question is, For how long? A few years? A few decades? Another half-century?

When change comes, will the new Chinese democrats thank companies like Google, Microsoft, Yahoo! and Cisco for bringing them the Internet as a catalyst for freedom? Or will they curse them for helping a corrupt and unaccountable regime hang on to power longer than it might have, thus ruining a lot of lives that might otherwise not have been ruined? Will the Chinese thank the American people for their support? Or will they mutter under their breath about hypocrites who talked a big game about freedom and democracy—but who weren't willing to forego a cent of profit to help non-Americans realize those ideals?

Helping Chinese Censors

On February 15 [2006], Google, Microsoft, Yahoo! and Cisco were called on the carpet in a Congressional hearing for aiding and abetting Chinese government efforts to censor the Internet, monitor its citizens and suppress dissent online. Representative

In 2006 Google was one of four major U.S. companies strongly criticized at a congressional hearing about the way it conducts business in China. Google enables the Chinese government to censor Internet content and to have access to users' private information.

Tom Lantos, a California Democrat, asked executives of some of the world's most powerful companies how they can possibly sleep at night. All four responded with variations on the following theme: The Chinese people are still better off because US companies engage with the Chinese market and connect China to the global Internet. They're doing their best to do the right thing, but it's impossible to keep your hands completely clean in a place like China. You still have to follow Chinese laws and regulations even if Chinese law enforcement is rather less accountable than back home.

    It's important to be clear—as many members of Congress at the hearings did not appear to be—that these four companies have all made different choices about their business practices in China. They fall at very different points along an "evil scale." Here's how they shake down:

- *Cisco* sells routers with censorship capability built into them, but the same technology is necessary to protect computer networks from viruses. It remains unclear exactly how much training and service Cisco knowingly provides to Chinese customers whose primary intent is to censor political speech. But meanwhile, it does acknowledge selling surveillance technologies directly to the Chinese Public Security Bureau and other law-enforcement bodies in a country where law enforcement is well documented to commit rampant human rights abuses. Cisco's excuse? Selling communications technology to these organizations is not against US law. If I were a Chinese dissident, I'd be grateful that Cisco had helped bring the Internet to China, but I'd also be outraged that Cisco may have helped the cops keep me under surveillance and catch me trying to organize protest activities.
- *Microsoft* provides instant messaging and Hotmail (hosted on servers outside China so it doesn't have to hand over data), as well as a Chinese version of MSN Spaces, which it censors in accordance with Chinese government requirements. So when Chinese blogger Zhao Jing wrote in support of fired newspaper editors in December, his blog got deleted. Now MSN has refined its censorship so that censored blogs only get blocked to Internet users inside China, while people in the rest of the world can still access the sites. Chinese bloggers report that a number of bloggers who have been writing in support of *Freezing Point*, a periodical that was recently shut down, have had their blogs censored by MSN. Zhao, one of the censored bloggers, wrote that while he's angry about the censorship, he still thinks that the majority of Chinese bloggers are better off with MSN Spaces than without it.
- *Yahoo!* has a Chinese-language portal hosted inside China, with a search engine that filters out all websites and keywords

deemed unacceptable by Chinese authorities. It does not inform users that the content is being censored in any way. Yahoo! also offers a Chinese-language e-mail service hosted on computer servers inside the People's Republic. Because the user data is under Chinese legal jurisdiction, Yahoo! is obligated to comply with Chinese police requests to hand over information. Such compliance over the past several years has led to the jailing of at least three dissidents. If I were one of those people or their loved ones, I would never forgive Yahoo!

- *Google* in January rolled out a new censored search engine, Google.cn. Some Chinese bloggers have mockingly called it the "eunuch" or "neutered" Google. However, Google executives point out that the site notifies users that their search results are censored, and that the uncensored Google.com remains accessible to Chinese. They also say they have decided not to provide Chinese e-mail or blog-hosting services in order to avoid putting themselves in the position that Yahoo! and Microsoft have found themselves in. If I were a Chinese user, I would give Google serious points for considering the human rights implications of its business decisions, and for trying hard to be as transparent and honest with the user as possible while still attempting to have a viable business in the People's Republic. I would not be happy, though, that Google has helped to legitimize political censorship as an accepted business practice.

Chinese Internet Users React

What do Chinese Internet users think? From reading the reaction of Chinese blogs over the past several weeks and talking to my friends back in China, it's pretty clear that most Chinese Internet users are indeed glad that Google searches remain available in China and that MSN Spaces still makes blogging so easy. But Yahoo! is taking a beating. Blogger Zhao Jing wrote: "A company such as Yahoo! which gives up information is unfor-

Internet Censorship: Who Controls What?

Countries that filter Internet content concerning politics, human rights, freedom of expression, minority rights, and religious freedom:

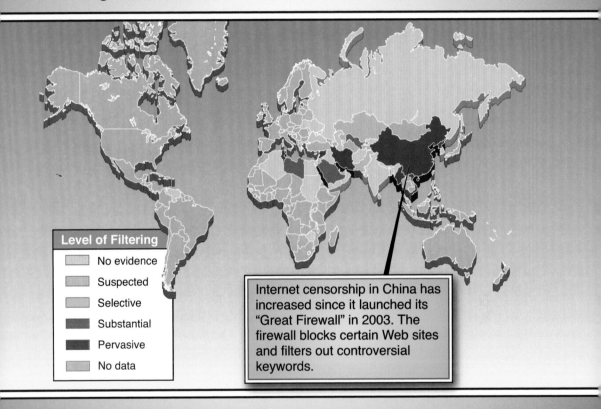

Level of Filtering
- No evidence
- Suspected
- Selective
- Substantial
- Pervasive
- No data

Internet censorship in China has increased since it launched its "Great Firewall" in 2003. The firewall blocks certain Web sites and filters out controversial keywords.

Taken from: Paddy Allen and Bobbie Johnson, "Internet Censorship: Who Controls What?" guardian.co.uk, June 30, 2009.

givable. It would be for the good of the Chinese netizens if such a company could be shut down or get out of China forever."

Immediately after the House hearings, draft legislation for the Global Online Freedom Act of 2006 was introduced in the House by New Jersey Republican Christopher Smith, with Tom Lantos as co-sponsor. The act aims to make it illegal for US companies to enable the suppression of online speech in China and in other countries where governments are not democratically accountable. It includes provisions that would forbid the storage of user data on servers inside China, would make it illegal to sell equipment or services to law enforcement agencies in countries like China and would enable victims of Yahoo!'s police collaboration to sue Yahoo! In US court. The specifics of these provisions will need to be substantially fine-tuned in order to insure that US companies can behave more ethically while not straitjacketing them to the point that they are unable to function. Representatives of Google, Microsoft and Yahoo! have all said they welcome US government action that would level the playing field and give them an excuse to give Chinese authorities for not complying with certain requests. If they are serious, they will work with Congress to shape these provisions so that they can not only pass but be possible to implement and enforce.

However, other provisions in the bill leave a lot of Americans and Chinese scratching their heads. The bill would require US Internet companies to hand over all lists of forbidden words provided to them by "any foreign official of an Internet-restricting country" (as defined by the US State Department) to a specially created US Office of Global Internet Freedom. It would also require these companies to report all content deleted or blocked at the request of such a government to the same government office. Free speech groups like the Electronic Frontier Foundation have pointed out that this would place US Internet companies in the position of acting as informers to the US government about actions of a foreign government. It also would result in handing over Chinese user information to the US government, which raises the question: Why should Chinese users be expected to trust the US government with their information, when many Americans don't trust their government with personal data? Why should Google hand over information on Chinese users to the US government when it is fighting requests from the US Department of Justice for data on its own citizens? Aren't we better off setting global standards to protect all users from all governments everywhere?

Respecting Chinese Rights

Chinese bloggers were encouraged by the Congressional hearings because they called attention to the evil effects of corporate censorship, surveillance and police collaboration. But they also found the hearings to be patronizing—based on the presumption that Americans have the power to change the Chinese political system if only we can pass enough laws. To quote Zhao Jing again: "The bill to be submitted about freedom of Internet information treats the freedom of Chinese Internet users as a slave girl to be dressed as you please."

We must not allow American companies to deprive Zhao and his generation of their right to shape their country's political future. But we must do it in a way that shows we respect the rights of the Chinese people—and the rights of every human being on the planet—as much as we respect our own.

Not only is this just the right thing to do: It will also increase the chances that future Chinese regimes will actually be friendly toward the United States, because the population voting them into office might actually stand a chance of being convinced that American people do care about something beyond our self-interest.

EIGHT

Internet Providers May Benefit More People by Working with Government Censors

PR Week

In the following viewpoint taken from an op-ed article in *PR Week*, a public relations professional in Beijing, China, argues that, despite the uproar surrounding Internet providers such as Google cooperating with the Chinese government, it would be a mistake for these companies to leave China. Some dissenting views are appearing in state-controlled publications, and journalists are beginning to serve as a check on the Chinese government. Also, the government cannot completely control the Internet access of all 110 million users in China, and many users are already accessing banned information. While the restrictions on freedom of the press and speech in China should be criticized, the country also needs support to move toward a more open society.

Much has been written recently about censorship in China and how US corporations doing business there should respond. First there was the uproar about Google, Yahoo, and others cooperating with the Chinese government by handing over

PR Week, "Op-Ed: China Requires Support to Evolve," March 20, 2006. Copyright © 2006 Haymarket Media, Inc. Reproduced by permission.

data and selling systems to restrict information on the Internet in China. Tom Lantos, the senior Democrat on the House International Relations Committee, chastised the companies for abetting the Chinese government's efforts to repress free speech. Then there was the furor over China's Communist Party shutting down Freezing Point, a weekly section of the China Youth Daily, for distributing a document that purportedly attacked the socialist system and criticized history textbooks used in Chinese schools.

Critics suggest that these episodes were just the latest examples of why US corporations should stop doing business in China. Pulling out of the country, they say, is the only way to pressure the regime to allow unfettered access to information. I'd like to

Google vice president Elliot Schrange (right) testifies before Congress about Google's role in the censorship practices of the Chinese government.

offer a brief perspective on these events as a PR pro [public relations professional] in Beijing who works for a global firm and believes it would be a mistake for companies to leave China.

The Tide Is Turning

First, there is no question that the Chinese government continues to hold tightly to a legacy of control over the flow of information. But the tide is turning—slowly, but positively. Courageous journalists, such as Freezing Point's Li Datong, are starting to question the government instead of serving as Party mouthpieces. And as any PR pro in China knows, 'guanxi,' or good connections, is less important in determining what gets covered in the Chinese press.

What's more, globalization has brought on enormous changes in just about every walk of life in China, including the media. While government controls remain in place, there is widespread coverage of dissenting views in state-controlled publications. Be it rural protests against official corruption, mismanagement at some of the country's largest corporations, or criticism of governments' economic policies, the Chinese media are now full of reports on subjects people were afraid to talk about only a decade ago. In turn, journalists in China are becoming more professional and beginning to serve as a check on government.

Second, as much as the Chinese government tries to control the Internet, it is impossible to do so completely. China now has the second-largest population of Internet users—110 million people—in the world and will likely overtake the US for the top spot in the near future. Chinese Internet users are extremely savvy about accessing banned information and frequently express their views on hitherto taboo subjects in chat rooms, discussion forums, and blogs; government measures to restrict access to specific Web sites and certain information have had little impact on this reality.

Western governments and media are right to criticize any restrictions on freedom of the press and speech in China. But more than ever, we in China need your encouragement as our country

Internet Censorship by Repressive Regimes

Percentage of Web sites in each category that were blocked in China, Iran, Saudi Arabia, Tunisia, and Burma.

	China	Iran	Saudi Arabia	Tunisia	Burma
Sites on Censor Circumvention	5%	95%	41%	87%	11%
Drugs	0%	0%	86%	0%	4%
E-mail Providers	10%	0%	0%	0%	85%
Gambling	8%	0%	93%	0%	24%
Gay/Lesbian	11%	11%	11%	11%	3%
Hate Speech	13%	4%	5%	4%	4%
Humor	0%	6%	37%	17%	0%
Sites on Major Historical Events	14%	0%	23%	0%	3%
News Outlets	6%	3%	0%	0%	8%
Porn	39%	100%	98%	95%	65%
Provocative Attire	6%	18%	18%	12%	0%
Sex Education	8%	4%	7%	0%	4%

Taken from: Matthew Quirk, "The Web Police," *Atlantic Magazine*, May 2006.

evolves toward a more open and transparent society. We need you to be good role models from whom we can learn best practices in journalism and PR.

What we don't need are self-righteous polemics and calls for boycotts. Such threats often backfire and may make the government even more recalcitrant. Balancing criticism with encouragement isn't easy, but it's crucial to the future of China—and to the world itself.

NINE

Television Content Should Not Be Censored

Trey Parker and Matt Stone, interviewed by Nick Gillespie and Jesse Walker

In the following interview with *South Park* creators Matt Stone and Trey Parker, *Reason* magazine writers Nick Gillespie and Jesse Walker discuss how censorship has impacted the popular program. Censorship issues came to the forefront in the 2006 season when Comedy Central began blocking specific content and in some cases refusing to re-air certain episodes. In one instance, Comedy Central told Stone and Parker that they would not air portions of an episode that featured a cartoon version of Muhammad. Stone and Parker, however, made the issue of censorship clear within the program, and the episode also became available later as an illegal download online. While Stone and Parker are fully aware of the limits regarding free expression on network television, they enjoy pushing against those limits to explore new issues.

South Park is many things. First and foremost, it is scabrously [scandalously] funny and antinomian [rejects socially established morality], taking laser-guided aim at targets ranging from the ridiculous—one episode mocked [directors] George Lucas'

Nick Gillespie and Jesse Walker, "South Park Libertarians: Trey Parker and Matt Stone on Liberals, Conservatives, Censorship, and Religion," *Reason*, vol. 38, December 1, 2006. Copyright © 2006 by Reason Foundation, 3415 S. Sepulveda Blvd., Suite 400, Los Angeles, CA 90034. www.reason.com. Reproduced by permission.

and Steven Spielberg's intentions to change the first *Raiders of the Lost Ark* movie for DVD release—to the sublime: In one particularly memorable episode from the first season, the *South Park* boys battle a Godzilla-like version of [actress/singer] Barbra Streisand with the aid of [actor] Sidney Poitier, film critic Leonard Maltin, and rock star Robert Smith of The Cure. (After that episode, by the way, Streisand attacked the show, not for showing her as a monster but for promoting cynicism among children.)

More commonly, though, the show takes on serious topics in a hilarious manner. These include idiotic sex and drug education programs foisted on kids who are smarter, or at least more sensible, than their parents and teachers, and moral panics over everything from video games to gay sex to environmental degradation. A recent episode featured former Vice President Al Gore dragging the town along on a feverish hunt for a mythical "ManBearPig." Another episode warns of a "smug alert" emanating from Hollywood after [actor] George Clooney's self-congratulatory speech at last year's Oscars. Simply put, for the last decade, *South Park* has produced the sharpest satire of American politics and culture. . . .

We'll talk to Trey and Matt about what it's like to take on the politics and attitudes of their peers in Hollywood, what their own politics are, and where those politics came from.

We'll also talk to them about religion. If lampooning self-important, self-indulgent celebrities—and it's not clear there is any other kind—is one constant on the show, so is skewering religious hypocrisy and extremism. In various episodes, Trey and Matt have taken on aspects of Judaism, Christianity, and Islam, and a conspicuously gay Satan is one of the more sympathetic characters in the *South Park* movie. Perhaps even more dangerously, they have made fun of the [litigious] Church of Scientology, a group that may not be as thick with suicide bombers as Islam but is certainly better represented by lawyers. . . .

South Park and Censorship

We're going to open things up, though, with a discussion of free speech and censorship issues. Never before in human history have we been more free to express ourselves, and never before have the opponents of free speech been more vocal and, in some instances, deadly.

In the United States, we've seen continuing and ramped-up attempts to extend government regulation of speech to cable and satellite TV and radio and to increase restrictions on unambiguously political speech via campaign finance "reform." In Europe, we've witnessed the rise not only of laws designed to spare the feelings of certain groups by shutting down "offensive" speech but death threats and actual murders of people who refuse to be silenced. One of the reasons we were interested in having a conference in Amsterdam is that it's not only the birthplace of tolerance but the site of one of the most brutal crimes related to free speech in recent memory: the 2004 murder of Dutch filmmaker Theo Van Gogh, who was stabbed to death in the street after making a 10-minute film critical of Islam's treatment of women.

So let's start off with a discussion of two recent episodes. In the wake of the violent reaction to the Muhammad cartoons that appeared in the Danish newspaper *Tyllands-Posten*[1], you wrote a story in which the Prophet appeared on the cartoon series *Family Guy*. Comedy Central refused to air the scene in which Muhammad actually appeared. You also recently produced an episode mocking [actor and Scientologist] Tom Cruise and Scientology, which the network refused to rerun earlier this year.

Reason: *So the first question is, what's more terrifying, crossing Islam or crossing Scientology?*

Trey Parker: They're really the same people.

This is what happened. I was on my honeymoon in Disney World. I turned on the television, and there were thousands of rioting Muslims, and the caption said, "Muslims enraged over cartoon." And I said, "Oh, shit. What did we do?"

We actually did an episode five years ago with Muhammad in it. It was an episode called "Super Best Friends," and Muhammad had super powers and turned himself into a beaver and then

1. The cartoons were published in the September 30, 2005, issue. Muslims protested the cartoons because they depicted the Islamic prophet Muhammad.

"What is the best way to censor TV?", cartoon by Fischer, Ed. www.cartoonstock.com.

killed Abraham Lincoln. I thought, "They finally just saw it, and they're all pissed off." But no, it was those other cartoons that they were mad about.

So Matt and I were like, "This is great; we have our first episode." Comedy Central kept saying, "We're not going to broadcast a Muhammad episode." And we said, "You totally have the right, it's your network, but we're going to make one, and it's going to be one of the seven you pay for."

Matt Stone: And then we made it two episodes out of seven.

It was life imitating art, because the whole week after the first one aired there was a teaser, "Will television executives take a stand for free speech? Or will Comedy Central puss out?" That whole week we were trying to get Comedy Central to show Muhammad. And they pussed out.

Reason: *They did show most of the episode, but they blocked out the specific moment when Muhammad appears. I know people who assumed you decided to run those title cards yourself, as part of the satire: "In this shot, Muhammad hands a football helmet to Family Guy. Comedy Central has refused to broadcast an image of Muhammad on their network."*

Stone: It was really hard to come up with the right approach. What do you do other than just put black and white cards up to say this isn't us, the network really wouldn't show this image, they really have been bullied into this? We toyed with the idea of putting some really incredible quote up or making a big speech. At the end of the day it felt a little too high and mighty, so we ended up doing the driest thing possible.

Reason: *Do you find yourself facing more restrictions on what you can do now or when you started out?*

Parker: It started last Christmas when we did an episode—it was really an episode about alcoholism, but it happened to have a statue of the Virgin Mary shitting blood on the Pope.

Stone: So it wasn't really about that.

Parker: Yeah. It was really saying these things about A.A. [Alcoholics Anonymous], but that was the first episode that a Catholic group got really upset about, and Comedy Central pulled it [from the rerun schedule]. We were like, "Wow, that's never happened." Then a few months after that, suddenly they were pulling the Tom Cruise episode.

On one hand, we're thinking, "We're living in a pretty different time now. All this stuff's getting pulled off the air." On the other hand, we're thinking, "Well, the Virgin Mary is shitting blood on the Pope."

Stone: Our point was that if you're going to pull this off for offending somebody, you don't have any episodes of *South Park* left. Somebody will complain about every single episode.

Reason: *When it looked like Comedy Central wasn't going to rerun the Mary episode, people were still able to download it illegally online. Did you see that as a victory for free speech, or did you think, "My God, these people are stealing our intellectual property"?*

Stone: We're always in favor of people downloading. Always.

Reason: *Why?*

Stone: It's how a lot of people see the show. And it's never hurt us. We've done nothing but been successful with the show. How could you ever get mad about somebody who wants to see your stuff?

Parker: We worked really hard making that show, and the reason you do it is because you want people to see it.

Reason: *How did other people in the creative community respond to your recent controversies?*

Parker: When we did the Muhammad episode, we got flowers from the *Simpsons* people because we ripped on *Family Guy*. Then we got calls from the *King of the Hill* people saying, "You're doing God's work ripping on *Family Guy*." Even though it was this big political thing about Muhammad and whatever, everyone was just, "Thank you for you ripping on *Family Guy*."

Reason: *Are you secretly hoping that radical Islamists, who are not always the closest readers of texts, will actually think Family Guy ran an episode showing Muhammad?*

Stone: Well, that's the other big joke. We really weren't that brave. If it did make it over to some obscure part of Pakistan, they'd be like, "Hey, we ought to kill the guys who did *Family Guy*."

Reason: *In the climactic scene of the episode, Kyle lectures the president of Fox that he has to stand up in favor of free speech. Is it true that the dialogue was taken directly from the conversations you had with Comedy Central about showing Muhammad?*

Stone: Yes, the dialogue is almost exactly the same. We even had Kyle call him Doug, right?

Stone: Doug Herzog is the head guy over at Comedy Central.

Parker: It was very personal.

Stone: At some point I think we knew we were going to lose. We weren't going to get Muhammad on, so we were just going to make them feel really bad about it. I mean, we've been at an ACLU [American Civil Liberties Union] meeting where we gave Doug an award for freedom of speech, and once you get an award for freedom of speech, you've got to step up to the plate.

Reason: *Talk a little bit about Tom Cruise and the Scientology episode.*

Parker: The quick summary is that one of the little boys, Stan, is told he should take a personality test by these people hanging out near the mall. He takes the test, and they inform him that he's really, really unhappy, which he didn't realize, and so they tell him all the steps he needs to go through to learn about Scientology. But then they have him do that thing they do in Scientology where they take your electrode readings and take you back in your childhood. He does that, and they realize his readings are so over the top that he must be the reincarnation of L. Ron Hubbard, so now he's actually not just in the cult; he's leading the cult. So everyone's descending on *South Park*, and of course Tom Cruise comes as well, wanting his approval.

Reason: *How did the network respond to pressure from the Church of Scientology about that episode?*

Stone: They blew it off. To be fair, it wasn't really at the Comedy Central level. It was way up at the Viacom level. [Viacom owns Comedy Central.] It wasn't a choice or anything we had any say in. The only thing that we got was a phone call saying

Matt Stone (left) and Trey Parker, creators of the irreverent South Park TV show, have had ongoing issues with the Comedy Central network's efforts to censor their show.

that the producers of *Mission Impossible: 3* [which stars Cruise] want this show off the air.

This was on a Wednesday. The rerun was supposed to air that night. So we bitched and moaned and yelled at them on the phone, and they said, "You may be mad about that, but what you're really going to be mad about is we don't want you to go to the press and say anything." That was really tough, because that felt like we were playing along with this, to me, fundamentally immoral organization like Scientology. But then we realized —and luckily it came true—that you can't just pull an episode off the air anymore. People are going to find out. Sure enough, it was all over the press. The Internet makes those backroom deals a lot harder to do.

Reason: *You have a money-making franchise, and you're built into a large multinational corporation's distribution channel. Do you feel more worried when you do something that might rock the boat?*

Parker: This last year has been a really amazing year. We've suddenly found ourselves back in the headlines again because of the shows we were doing. It wasn't an intentional thing. It was just that we've reached that level now where we're very comfortable saying, "You know what? We're done. We've made all the money we need, and we both have always had dreams of doing other things." As soon as they say, "We're not going to let you do a Muhammad episode," we can say, "All right, well, we're not going to do any more shows for you this season."

Stone: They were really bummed out when we called them and said we're going to do a Muhammad episode. They're like, "Ahh, f---. Oh my God, you guys." Because they can't tell us no. A smaller show, they would've just said, "No, you can't do it. End of story." And a bigger show like *The Simpsons* wouldn't dare risk their franchise. It's such a stupid political move, but we're just stupid enough to do it.

Reason: *This is a bizarre time to be alive. You have places like YouTube, where you can create whatever you want and disseminate it. At the same time, you have lawsuits, and you have people literally being killed. So what's the state of free expression?*

Stone: We obviously have a very one-sided view of it. Basically all we've ever done is said what we wanted to say, and people have just thrown money at us. We would love to be very [filmmaker] Michael Moore and go out there and go, "Yeah, they're trying to quiet us." Because that immediately gets people on your side.

People ask, "So how is it working for a big multinational conglomeration?" I'm like, "It's pretty good, you know? We can say whatever we want. It's not bad. I mean, there are worse things." It doesn't mean that we don't have battles like we did this year, where you get really frustrated with the fact that *Mission Impossible:3*'s bigger than *South Park* and they can shut you down, but at the end of the day you've got to look at the balance sheet.

Parker: At the end of the day, they gave us $40 million for a puppet movie.

Reason: *You did an episode where the boys encountered the Knights of Standards and Practices, who explained why they shouldn't say shit on television. At face value, that story seems to say that there are proper limits to what you can put on TV. Are there limits that you won't cross?*

Parker: Totally. But year after year, it's always a different thing. When we look at the shows we were doing years ago—to think that people were freaking out over these episodes! If you look at our first season now, you could put it on PBS next to *Sesame Street*.

Stone: They're like cute little Teletubbies.

Parker: They're just cute little kids. "Oh, he's farting fire, that's cute."

It's not that every year we get together and go, "How can we push it more?" But the boundaries are part of the fun, and the fact that it's on television is part of the fun of what we're getting away with.

Stone: And then, when we did the *South Park* movie, we changed what the limits were because they're different for movies than for TV.

TEN

Television Content Should Be Censored

Parents Television Council

> The Parents Television Council is a nonpartisan education organization advocating responsible entertainment. In 2007–2008, the Parents Television Council in partnership with Enough Is Enough, a campaign to stem societal violence, collected data relating to three television programs, *Rap City* and *106 & Park* on BET and *Sucker Free* on MTV. The two organizations referred to the content that was viewed on all programs as vulgar and offensive. Furthermore, the survey revealed that neither BET nor MTV—with one exception—included program descriptions that would have allowed these shows to be blocked by V-chips. The Parents Television Council and Enough Is Enough reported finding explicit sexual content, violent images, and obscene language in each of the three programs and accused both BET and MTV of frequently rating each network's programming incorrectly. The Parents Television Council believes that parents need to monitor what their children watch on television and must demand more accountability from networks.

The Parents Television Council™ (PTC), in partnership with the Enough is Enough Campaign, released shocking

Parents Television Council, "Children Assaulted by Sex, Violence, Drugs and Explicit Language on BET and MTV," April 10, 2008. Copyright © 1998–2006 Parents Television Council. All rights reserved. Reproduced by permission.

new data about BET [Black Entertainment Television] and MTV [Music Television], daytime music video programming. As recently as March 2008, children who watched BET's *Rap City* and *106 & Park* and MTV's *Sucker Free* on MTV were bombarded with adult content—sexual, violent, profane or obscene —once every 38 seconds.

"What BET and MTV are offering to children on these three programs is full of offensive and vulgar content, the likes of which cannot yet be found on broadcast television. Being in the trenches fighting for better indecency enforcement and cable choice on behalf of millions of American families, we thought we'd seen it all—but even we were taken aback by what we found in the music video programs on MTV and BET that are targeted directly at impressionable children," PTC President Tim Winter said.

Inexcusable Content

"BET and MTV are assaulting children with content that is full of sexually charged images, explicit language, portrayals of violence, drug use, drug sales and other illegal activity. Not only that, but we discovered that some offensive words aired only in muted form in December 2007, but as recent as March 2008, these same words were not muted.

"Excluding one program on BET, neither BET or MTV carried content descriptors that would work in conjunction with the V-Chip to block the programs from coming into the home or to warn parents about the presence of sexual content, suggestive dialogue, violence, or foul language. This is a major problem for parents who are told repeatedly to rely on their V-chips to protect their children," said Winter.

In a report prepared for the Enough is Enough Campaign, the PTC analyzed adult content airing on BET's *Rap City* and *106 & Park* and on MTV's *Sucker Free* on MTV for a two-week period in December 2007. These shows were chosen due to their daily new and recent video releases. The content analyzed aired during afternoon or early evening hours, when many children are at home after school. Because the research data from the December content contained a strikingly high volume and degree of adult-themed material, the PTC conducted an additional week of analysis on the same three programs in March 2008 for purposes of validation. The data revealed even higher levels of adult content in March 2008 than in December 2007.

Major Findings:

- The PTC documented 1,647 instances of offensive/adult content in the 27.5 hours of programming analyzed during the December 2007 study period, for an average of 59.9 instances per hour, or nearly one instance every minute.

The Parents Television Council and the organization Enough Is Enough, after collecting data on several TV shows, including MTV's Sucker Free, reported that these programs presented highly adult material during the day.

- In March 2008, there were 1,342 instances of offensive/adult content in a mere 14 hours of programming, or 95.8 instances per hour, 1.6 instances per minute, or one instance of adult content every 38 seconds.
- To put this data in perspective, in the PTC's most recent analysis of prime time broadcast TV Family Hour programming, the data revealed an average 12.5 instances of violent, profane and sexual content per hour. This is equivalent to one instance every 4.8 minutes.
- Most of what children are seeing in these music videos are sexually charged images—45% of the adult content in the analyzed videos was of a sexual nature, followed by explicit language (29%), violence (13%), drugs use/sales (9%), and other illegal activity (3%). Although March data revealed higher quantities of content, the percentages represented similar findings (42%, 37%, 10%, 9% and 2% respectively).
- The PTC documented 746 sexually explicit scenes or lyrical references in the 27.5 hours of analyzed programming from the December study period for an average of 27 instances per hour, or one instance every 2.2 minutes. Sexual content was even more common in the March test period, with an average 40 instances per hour, or one instance every 90 seconds.
- With respect to language, the PTC documented 475 uses of explicit language and obscene gestures in December for an average of 17 instances per hour, or one instance every 3.5 minutes, and 495 uses of explicit language and obscene gestures in March, for an average of 35 instances per hour, or one instance every 1.7 minutes.
- The most commonly used expletive during both the December and March study period was (muted) "n-word," which artists verbalized 148 times within a two-week period in December and verbalized 136 times within the one-week study period in March.
- Vulgar slang references to sexual anatomy increased from a mere 3 instances in December to 103 references in the

one-week March test period. Other categories of sexual content, such as direct/non-slang references to sex and depictions of strippers also increased dramatically.

- From the December broadcasts, the PTC documented 221 depictions of violence, including deaths depicted or implied, explosions, implied violence, punching/hitting, rioting, threats and weapons; this data equates to an average of 8 instances per hour, or one instance roughly every 7.5 minutes. Violence also became more frequent in the March analysis, averaging one instance every 6.3 minutes.
- Of the violent content in the videos analyzed, 55% included the use or depiction of weapons, the second largest category of violence was deaths depicted or implied (16%), followed by threats of violence (11%).
- The PTC also documented 205 depictions or discussions of drug sale or use and other illegal activity during the study period, for an average of 7.5 instances per hour, or roughly one instance every eight minutes. The depiction of illegal narcotic use or sale dominated this category—75% of references to or depictions of illegal activity in the analyzed videos were drug-related.
- All episodes of *Sucker Free* on MTV included in this analysis were rated TV-14. By contrast, almost every episode of *106 & Park* and *Rap City* on BET carried only a TV-PG rating. An exception was found with one show that aired in December, which was rated TV-14 and included descriptors for suggestive dialogue, foul language, and sex.
- During the two-week December 2007 study period, children under 18 made up approximately 40% of the viewing audience for *106 & Park*, 41% of the audience for *Rap City* and 39% of the audience for *Sucker Free* on MTV. Because all of these programs re-air throughout the day, study results underestimate the percentage of unique children who are exposed or have been exposed to these programs in total.

"There are several solutions. First of all, parents need to be more involved in monitoring their children's media consumption, establishing and sticking to household rules about media

Pickles

"Pickles" used with permission of Brian Crane and The Washington Post Writers Group in Conjunction with the Cartoonist Group. All rights reserved.

use, and discussing media content with their children. Advertisers need to be held accountable for the content their advertising dollars pay for. Those companies that advertise on programs like *106 & Park, Rap City,* and *Sucker Free* on MTV can and should use their unique influence with BET and MTV to push for greater responsibility where program content is concerned," Winter said.

"Consumers must demand and receive the right to pick and choose—and pay for—only the cable channels they want coming into their homes. It is unconscionable that parents who wish to protect their children from this content are nonetheless forced to subsidize it with their cable subscription dollars. Finally, we must demand from the networks an accurate, transparent, and consistent ratings system that will give parents adequate tools to protect their children from inappropriate content.

"Today is just the first step towards making progress and we commend Pastor Delman Coates, founder of the Enough is Enough Campaign, and those who work with him for demanding change and accountability from BET and MTV. It takes the courage of concerned citizens to speak out against destructive images on television and to see change happen," Winter concluded.

ELEVEN

Some Laws Against Hate Speech Could Threaten Free Speech

Peter Tatchell

In the following article from *The Guardian* (London), human rights activist Peter Tatchell wonders whether a new law penalizing hate speech against homosexuals will be helpful. He says one problem is that the law singles out homosexuals, when in truth any hate speech directed at any person or group should be equally offensive before the law. Another problem, according to Tatchell, is that these kinds of laws frequently infringe freedom of speech. In Australia, for instance, a man was arrested for displaying a sign offensive to the gay community. While people should certainly object to offensive opinions, Tatchell maintains that outlawing free expression may cause even more social conflicts. He contends the bigger problem, however, is not the need for a new law, but the need to enforce old laws against inciting violence. According to Tatchell, until the British authorities begin enforcing these laws, it makes little sense to pass new legislation.

[British politician] Jack Straw has decided to introduce yet another criminal offence, adding to the 3,000 new crimes Labour has introduced since it came to power in 1997. This latest offence will prohibit the incitement of homophobic hatred.

Peter Tatchell, "Hate Speech v. Free Speech," *Guardian*, October 10, 2007. Copyright © 2007 Guardian Newspapers Limited. Reproduced by permission of Guardian News Service, LTD.

It is intended to help tackle anti-queer prejudice, which is a good intention. But will this legislation work? Is it necessary? Might it not lead to infringements of free speech? Are there more effective ways to challenge homophobia and other hateful incitements?

A much more important issue is the fact that the government, police and prosecution service are failing to enforce the laws prohibiting the incitement of actual violence and murder against the lesbian, gay, bisexual and transgender communities. Inciting violence and murder is much worse, in my view, than inciting hate. Yet the relevant laws are often not enforced. Why not?

Equality Before the Law

On the positive side, the proposed new legislation will bring the statutes governing incitements to hatred on the ground of sexual orientation into line with the long-standing laws prohibiting the incitement of hate based on a person's race. In other words, it will establish parity in law with regard to stirring up hatred. But only partially. Many forms of incitement to hatred will continue to not be covered by criminal sanctions. These include incitements to hatred against asylum seekers, women, disabled people, travellers, ex-prisoners, people with HIV and so on.

If there are going to be laws against inciting hatred, they should be universal and prohibit all incitements to hatred—not just some. Singling out race hate and homo hate for special legal penalties strikes me as unfair and undesirable. It creates resentment among social groups who are not protected by such laws, which is bad for community cohesion. My view is very simple: everyone should be equal before the law, in which case all incitements of hatred should be an offence.

There are sound arguments to justify a prohibition on inciting hatred against vulnerable minorities who have a history of suffering persecution and prejudice. It is deemed to be a method of protecting them and creating a social atmosphere where they have redress against their tormentors.

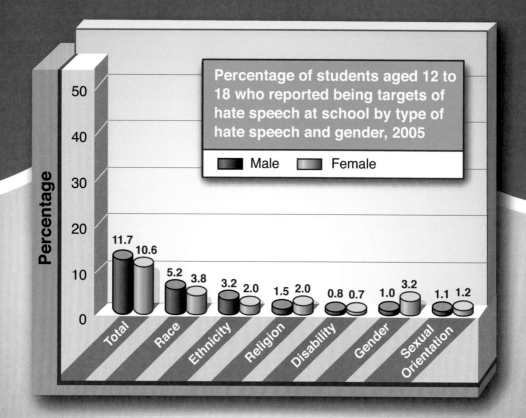

Hate Speech at School

Percentage of students aged 12 to 18 who reported being targets of hate speech at school by type of hate speech and gender, 2005

■ Male   ▢ Female

Type	Male	Female
Total	11.7	10.6
Race	5.2	3.8
Ethnicity	3.2	2.0
Religion	1.5	2.0
Disability	0.8	0.7
Gender	1.0	3.2
Sexual Orientation	1.1	1.2

Taken from: R. Dinkes, E.F. Cataldi, G. Kena, K. Baum, K. Baum, and T.D. Snyder, "Indicators of School Crime and Safety," U.S. Department of Education and Justice. Washington, DC: U.S. Government Printing Office.

Another argument, for which I have considerable sympathy, is that hatred is the gateway to discrimination, harassment and violence. It is the psychological foundation for serious, harmful criminal acts. Without the precondition of hatred, there would be no hate-motivated violent attacks on the black, Jewish and gay communities. In other words, if we can stop hatred and hate-mongers, we will stop the prejudice that often spills over into hateful, damaging acts, such as racist and queer-bashing murders. On these grounds, laws against inciting hatred are ethically justified and have practical benefits.

Infringing Freedom of Speech

The downside of incitement to hatred prohibitions is that they risk infringing freedom of speech. Who decides what constitutes hatred? It is a grey, disputable area. Defining hatred is difficult to determine in a way that will satisfy everyone. Different people have different interpretations of hatred. Is causing offence, or even distress, an incitement to hatred? What about ridiculing and mocking someone's beliefs? Is that hateful? Where do you draw the line between legitimate robust criticism and satire, and illegitimate, criminal incitement of hatred? It isn't simple and straightforward.

In 2007 a British law introduced to prohibit inciting homophobic hatred raised concerns about its possible infringement on free speech.

Many people say that these concerns are unfounded. They point to Ireland which has had comprehensive legislation banning the incitement of hatred since 1989. The law has been applied lightly and there has been no crackdown on free speech. It is said that the police and courts in the UK [United Kingdom] would show similar restraint. They will only go after the most excessively hateful and damaging incitements.

But can we be so sure? After all, similar laws have been abused in the recent past. An Oxford student was arrested and fined under the laws against public disorder for making a joke about a policeman's horse being gay. The officers construed this joke as a homophobic remark and nailed the student under the already existing wide-sweep public order legislation which bans behaviour likely to cause harassment, alarm or distress. It is not clear whether it was the police officer or the horse that was supposedly offended by the student's off-the-cuff quip.

Overzealous Laws

In the Australian state of Victoria, the law banning incitement to religious hatred has led to Christians and Muslims accusing one another of inciting hatred and bringing legal actions against each other, which has only served to inflame community relations.

In Bournemouth, the lay preacher, Harry Hammond, was convicted in 2001 under the public order laws for holding up a sign saying "Stop homosexuality, stop lesbianism." His arrest and conviction was, I believe, an outrageous infringement of free speech. Harry was, of course, a notorious homophobe. His prejudice needed to be rebutted, but not by making him a criminal and a martyr.

The same goes for all prejudice, whatever the motive and whoever the perpetrator. The best way to tackle prejudice is by presenting facts and using reasoned arguments, to break down ignorance and ill-will.

All incitements to hatred should be treated with the same zero tolerance. But not, in my opinion, by means of criminal sanctions. Free speech is precious. It should be limited only in exceptional circumstances—when it slips into inciting violence and murder.

The most effective way to diffuse hatred is by education and debate. Our schools, media and public figures have a vital role to play in challenging bigotry, encouraging social solidarity and helping to promote understanding and empathy with others.

Prevention is better than cure. Education and debate seeks to prevent hatred in the first place, whereas criminalisation seeks to punish the offender after he or she has already stirred hatred. It is shutting the stable door after the horse has bolted.

My real gripe is that inciting violence is much more serious than inciting hatred. Yet the laws prohibiting the advocacy and encouragement of homophobic violence are often not enforced.

Inciting Violence

For nearly two decades, despite repeated appeals from the gay community, the government, police and prosecution service have allowed record stores and radio stations to promote "murder music" songs inciting the killing of queers. Jamaican artists such as Buju Banton, Beenie Man and Bounty Killa have released CDs that openly encourage and glorify the shooting, burning, hanging and drowning of gay and lesbian people.

Inciting murder is a criminal offence under long-standing laws. Yet these songs have been given airplay on mainstream radio stations such as the BBC [British Broadcasting Corporation], as well as on local black pirate stations. The tracks are sold openly in many record stores and via online websites such as Amazon. The police have made no attempt to take action against the record companies and distributors, the record stores and websites, and the radio stations and deejays.

The police and Crown Prosecution Service (CPS) would never take such a hands-off approach to people who incited violence against black or Jewish people. Why the double standards?

Likewise, some fundamentalist Muslim clerics, on the extremist wing of Islam, openly urge the killing of gay people, unchaste women and Muslims who turn away from their faith. In east London in 2005, hate preacher Abdul Muhid of the pro-jihad Saviour Sect, urged the murder of homosexuals. Despite witnesses willing to go to court, the Crown Prosecution Service refused to prosecute him. Yet when the Islamist Abdullah el-Faisal incited the murder of Jews, Hindus and Americans in 2003 he was promptly arrested, convicted and jailed. More double standards.

The non-prosecution of Muslim clerics who incite the murder of gay people is a tragic betrayal of vulnerable gay and lesbian Muslims. They live in fear of the homophobic violence that is being stirred up by Islamist extremists. What signal does this official hands-off attitude send to queer Muslims? That the government does not care about their suffering? Police and CPS inaction gives homophobic persecutors a de facto green light to continue their violent threats.

Introducing legislation prohibiting the incitement of homophobic hatred seems a bit amiss when already-existing laws are not being enforced against the much more serious crimes of inciting violence and murder. Please, Mr Straw, ensure the enforcement of the current laws before you start introducing new ones.

TWELVE

Publishers Practice Self-Censorship of Young Adult Books

Patty Campbell

Patty Campbell has written about young adult literature for *Horn Book Magazine*. In her final column, she writes about the use of obscene words, specifically the f-word, in young adult books. More frequently than in the past, she believes, young adult books are being censored but not by the government. Instead, they are being censored by publishers and even the authors themselves, Campbell states. Many publishers, she maintains, would rather not censor young adult books but realize that if certain words appear in print, the book will be less likely to be used in school classrooms and libraries. Authors themselves, she states, are also agreeing to these changes to avoid controversy. Ironically, public libraries and bookstores have expressed less concern with censorship. This has created a dichotomy of two kinds of young adult books, one with no obscene words for the school market, and another with many obscene words for public libraries and bookstores.

Yesterday I googled the f-word. For a perfectly legitimate reason: I wanted some enlightenment on the growing paradox in YA lit [young adult literature] of both a wider usage of and a

Patty Campbell, "The Pottymouth Paradox," *Horn Book Magazine*, vol. 83, May/June, 2007, pp. 311–15. Copyright 2007 by The Horn Book, Inc., Boston, MA. www.hbook.com. All rights reserved. Reproduced by permission.

narrower tolerance for obscenity. Searches on terms such as profanity, censorship, obscenity, even bad words, had been uninformative, and so I punched up the Big Daddy of swear words in English. A testament to the power of that word is the way the search made me feel paranoid and perverted—as if I might end up on a government list somewhere. After surviving the predictable onslaught of porn sites, I discovered a treasure: a long, thoughtful (but entertaining) academic article by Christopher M. Fairman of the Ohio State Moritz College of Law, examining the legal implications and the power of the word, drawing on the research of etymologists, linguists, lexicographers, psychoanalysts, and social scientists. Among other fascinating data, he reveals that the earliest citations of the word go back to the fifteenth century, and even then the word appears encoded, in the way that contemporary writers less foolhardy than Fairman resort to f--k. The title of the piece, of course, is F---.

In this column, let us use the word as a marker for the pitifully sparse vocabulary of obscenity and profanity in written English, although the growing numbers of standard-bearers for word purity can even raise objections to proper names for body parts, like scrotum, as demonstrated by the brouhaha over this year's Newbery winner [Susan Patron's *The High Power of Lucky*]. And certainly censorship is a much more complex dilemma than just reactions to bad language."

"Bad" Words and Publishing

However, Fairman goes straight to the root of the problem as it is acted out in many a censorship battle over young adult literature: "F--- is a taboo word. The taboo is so strong that it compels many to engage in self-censorship. This process of silence then enables small segments of the population to manipulate our rights under the guise of reflecting a greater community." And yet despite the ever-increasing vigilance of these "small segments of the population," the language in some YA novels gets raunchier and raunchier. Take just one example from last year's crop, *Nick & Norah's Infinite Playlist*, by Rachel Cohn and

According to the viewpoint author, the book Nick &
Norah's Infinite Playlist, by Rachel Cohn and David
Levithan (pictured), is but one of many for young adults
that includes numerous obscene words.

David Levithan. In the book's first two chapters alone, the word f--- appears twenty-two times, other obscenities twenty-five times. And that's not unusual, as any reader of YA novels will testify. Of course, in this story about the inner workings of the punk-rock music scene, as in novels about war or urban poverty or deeply troubled teens, such language is completely appropriate for veracity and accurately reflects the characters' speech.

At the same time such YA novels are being accepted with hardly a blink, a single damn can be enough to disqualify a title for school or book club purchase. Why is this part of the YA market so much more sensitive to spicy language? According to [writer] Shannon Maughan, in a recent *Publishers Weekly* article:

> School library materials traditionally come under more scrutiny than those at public libraries, for a variety of reasons. School librarians are usually working within a smaller budget than their public library counterparts and have an additional duty to support the school's curriculum as well as answer to school administrators. This frequently means tighter guidelines for purchasing fiction. In addition, because students in a school setting are a more "captive" audience than patrons of a public library, the materials that students have access to at school are usually more closely monitored by parents.

Well aware of these factors, many school librarians and teachers are more vigilant than ever about selecting materials that will not raise parental or community concern. Unfortunately, such vigilance can lead to self-censorship that keeps books from getting onto, or remaining on, school library shelves.

Publishers and Censorship

Publishers, of course, are well aware of which of their books should be tidied up for possible school purchase. I have heard recently from several YA authors who have agreed to requests from their editors to change one or two words in a book so that it would qualify for acceptance in these less tolerant but lucrative markets. Sometimes this request comes from the book club or book fair managers. Occasionally only the library edition is expurgated, and the trade copy retains the offensive word (collectors take note). Or if the deal is negotiated after the book has been published, the book fair may take on the paperback rights and reprint the cleaned-up book themselves.

In a recent visit to the Kerlan Collection of Children's Literature at the University of Minnesota, I found evidence of many editorial discussions with authors about obscenities. A consistent theme was the editor's apologetic embarrassment about asking for language revisions. A letter from Atheneum editor Ginee Seo to author Chris Lynch about his 2005 novel *Inexcusable* vividly illustrates just how difficult this area is for editors committed to free expression:

> And—take a deep breath here—I cleaned up the language. This was a really difficult thing to do, as I think you can understand. Believe me, I agonized over this. I don't, as a rule, like to do this on young adult books. I don't want to compromise on how kids really talk. I don't want to acknowledge those f---ing gatekeepers. But in this case, Chris, I feel the book is so important—the message it's sending to young men so crucial—that I feel very strongly that this is a book that can and should be used in schools, and therefore I want to give it every advantage. You will say, okay, but won't some schools turn away from the book because of the subject matter anyway? Yes, some of them will. But other schools won't— and I don't want to make the argument for using the book that much harder for the teachers who decide to take it on. And if that means taking out a few f---s and shits from the narrative, I can live with that—and hope you can, too. Well, think about it, anyway.

Recently, Elizabeth Bicknell, editorial director of Candlewick Press, talked with me about her similar difficulties in striving for written speech that accurately reflects the characters without limiting the book's availability. Most spectacular was

Librarians Speak Out About Motivation for Self-Censorship

Which of the following has influenced your decision NOT to purchase a book?

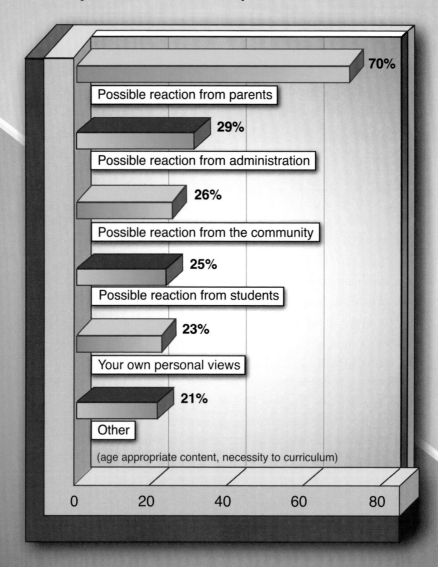

70% — Possible reaction from parents

29% — Possible reaction from administration

26% — Possible reaction from the community

25% — Possible reaction from students

23% — Your own personal views

21% — Other
(age appropriate content, necessity to curriculum)

0   20   40   60   80

Taken from: Debra Lau Whelan, "SLJ Self-Censorship Survey," *School Library Journal*, February 1, 2009.

the edit on Adam Rapp's *33 Snowfish*. Originally, she says, "the language was a lot stronger"—a possibility readers of this gritty novel will find hard to imagine. Bicknell toned the wording down to where she herself felt comfortable with it. Interestingly, it was not the big F and its variants but more colorful slang that she found disquieting. Rapp had said that releasing profanity allowed him to release the truth, but he and Bicknell found that when the profanity was later removed, the truth remained.

Bicknell also revealed that when Ron Koertge's *Brimstone Journals* was accepted by the Junior Literary Guild in 2001, it was the first time that august body had ever sponsored a book with f--- in its pages. Later, Koertge, perhaps made cautious by this near squeak, took all the "bad language" out of his spring 2007 novel *Strays*, then put it back when Bicknell felt that the sanitized book had lost its punch. Just this year, editor Deborah Noyes's fall 2007 short-story collection. *The Restless Dead* was nixed by the Guild until one f---ing was removed. But through all these negotiations, Bicknell asserts one overriding principle: "It's always the author's choice."

A Developing Dichotomy

Books that have no expectation of school or book club purchase can, and do, reach out freely to all the unlimited possibilities of the English language as it is spoken in many different places and situations. When the forces of "language purity" come across such books, they wallow in their outrage and strategize how to keep them away from readers. A spectacular example is PABBIS (Parents Against Bad Books in Schools), whose website reproduces the naughty bits in young adult books, sometimes pages and pages from a single novel, so that heavy-breathing would-be censors can read all the dirty parts without the bother of reading the book, and then follow the website's instructions on how to get the book banned.

We seem to have a dichotomy developing here. On the one hand are the "f----free" books with potential for book clubs and school libraries, and on the other are the "chock-full-o'-f---"

books more accepted by bookstores and public libraries. Quality is not a related factor; award books can come from either sector. Perhaps, if we are careful to be clear about its shape, this dichotomy is not a bad thing. Freedom of expression is readily available to authors, and those buyers who prefer books without swear words can have their books, too.

In case I've given the impression that this is a new problem in YA lit, let me hark back to one of the very first columns I wrote for the *Wilson Library Bulletin*, in 1978. In it I gave what I thought was a negative review of Kin Platt's *The Doomsday Gang*. Talking about its language, I said, "Not only do four-letter words appear on every page, they appear in nearly every sentence, and in their variant forms they substitute for almost any noun, verb, or adjective. The effect . . . is numbing. . . . But saying 'Goodness gracious!' instead of 'What the f---!' is opting for dishonesty." The passionate reactions from *Bulletin* readers, both pro and con, went on in the "Letters to the Editor" pages for five months.

So now I've ended my last column, as I began one of my first, with plentiful invocation of the f-word. If some *Horn Book* readers are enlightened or outraged, I welcome your letters as a farewell gift to the adversarial nature of "The Sand in the Oyster" [the title of the column]. YA lit, like teens themselves, is inherently controversial. In this long series of columns that began in 1993 I have tried to address some of those controversies as they arose, and to describe the genre as it developed. I have attempted to produce a body of criticism that would define the shape and boundaries and glories of young adult literature. Throughout this endeavor the *Horn Book* editors, especially Roger Sutton, have been supportive and provocative in productive ways, and I thank them. And so I leave my "Oyster" to make room for more varied voices on the exciting new developments in the genre, with hopes that there is a pearl somewhere to be found from these thirteen years of fishing for truth.

THIRTEEN

Free Expression Is Limited in the American Workplace

Bruce Barry

In the introduction to his book *Speechless: The Erosion of Free Expression in the American Workplace*, Bruce Barry, professor of management and sociology at Vanderbilt University, expresses his concern that American workers are losing their right to free speech in the workplace. Most Americans, he states, grow up accepting freedom of speech as a given right. While freedom of speech is theoretically protected from government interference, however, the private sector has no obligation to protect the First Amendment in the workplace. In a number of cases, Barry notes, employers have been willing to censor both employees' speech and political activities that fall outside of the workplace. In fact, he was motivated to write *Speechless* because often little recourse is available to those employees who have been censored in the workplace, and too few consequences are imposed on the employers who censor them. In essence, Barry writes, an employer has the right to control a worker's speech on and off the job without any due process, diminishing the rights of all American citizens.

Bruce Barry, *Speechless: The Erosion of Free Expression in the American Workplace*. San Pablo, CA: Berrett-Koehler Publishers, Inc., 2007. Copyright © 2007 by Bruce Barry. Reproduced by permission of Berrett-Koehler Publishers, Inc., San Francisco, CA. All rights reserved. www.bkconnection.com.

Imagine it's the fall of 2004. You arrive at the office building where you work and park in the parking lot. As you get out of your car and head to the building, you see your boss getting out of her car nearby and exchange a wave. Later that day she asks you to stop by her office, where she says, "Hey, I noticed when you pulled in this morning that [George W.] Bush-for-President sticker on your car. I don't know anything about your politics, but frankly I can't cope with having someone work for me who thinks Bush should be reelected. I'm sorry it's come to this, but you're fired. I need you to clear out by the end of the day."

Is this restriction on freedom of speech legal? Ethical? Reasonable? Outrageous?

What it isn't is far-fetched. It happened, with some minor variations, to Lynne Gobbell, an Alabama factory worker. Gobbell had a [presidential candidate] John Kerry bumper sticker. Her boss informed her that the owner of the factory, Phil Geddes, had demanded that she remove the sticker or be fired; he also told her, "you could either work for him or John Kerry." Geddes had on a previous occasion inserted a flyer in employee paycheck envelopes pointing out the positive effects that Bush's policies as president were having on them. "It upset me and made me mad," said Gobbell, "that he could put a letter in my check expressing his political opinion, but I can't put something on my car expressing mine."

Lynne Gobbell's experience, although striking and lamentable, is uncommon. If it were an everyday occurrence, she probably wouldn't have received a sympathetic phone call a few days later from John Kerry and an offer of a paid position with the Kerry campaign. Few people, even among those generally sympathetic to the management side of workplace issues, would likely view this as a great moment in the annals of employment or a wise use of managerial discretion. Even fewer would see it as a highlight in the history of free speech and the First Amendment.

Taking Free Speech for Granted

Americans take freedom of speech for granted. This attitude begins at an early age, in elementary and middle school, when students are first exposed to core principles of liberty embedded within the Constitution and the Bill of Rights. "Hey, it's a free country," we learn to say reflexively when others say or do harmlessly objectionable things. The term "free speech" becomes an easy defensive gambit when self-expression is challenged or silenced. After all, it's not just any individual right; it's at the heart of the *First* Amendment and the first of four "essential human freedoms" Franklin D. Roosevelt famously listed in his 1941 State of the Union speech. Justice Benjamin Cardozo in a 1937 Supreme Court opinion called it "the matrix, the indispensable condition, of nearly every other form of freedom." Writing more recently (if with similar extravagance), constitutional scholar David Strauss of the University of Chicago dubbed the First Amendment "the most celebrated text in all of American law."

We don't, for the most part, think much about why free speech matters, nor do we spend a lot of time thinking about the limits of free speech; we tend to leave that to lawyers and judges. Every so often, though, free speech comes center stage in the collective American mind for a while, usually when some national event or high-profile court case makes headlines. The aftermath of September 11, 2001, is a powerful example: A sudden onset of belligerence against a largely unseen "enemy" ignited a national conversation about the tension between liberty and security. Free speech is an important part of that conversation, as we learned painfully on September 26, 2001, shortly after 9/11. White House press secretary Ari Fleischer, near the end of his regular press briefing, was asked for a reaction to an acerbic [harsh] statement that the liberal comedian and provocateur Bill Maher had made about terrorists and the U.S. military. With an apparently contemptuous sneer at the First Amendment, Fleischer characterized Maher's comment as a reminder "to all Americans that they need to watch what they say, watch what they do. This is not a time for remarks like that; there never is."

The First Amendment does not, of course, generally require that people "watch what they say," even in times of military engagement, and Fleischer's comment was rightly pilloried [ridiculed]. (So was the shabby attempt by Fleischer's office to rewrite history by initially leaving the words "watch what they say" out of the White House's official briefing transcript.) The reality, though, is that people frequently do watch what they say, not because the law requires it, but because life requires it. The great thing about our constitutional system of free speech is that personal expression is presumptively safe from government interference. But the flip side is that personal expression is safe *only* from government interference. Our system of constitutional law generally fails to protect civil liberties, including free speech, from actions that threaten or infringe upon them when those actions are committed by private parties. Employers in the private sector have no obligation to respect the expressive rights or impulses of those who work for them. Even in public-sector jobs, where government is the employer, the reach of the First Amendment is quite limited. At work, Fleischer's dictum is fully realized: we must watch what we say.

Censoring Employees

Although what happened to Lynne Gobbell—losing a job over a bumper sticker—may not be typical, it is one of the extreme cases that define the subject because they vividly illustrate the abundant power available to employers for controlling the expressive activities of employees. Extreme cases also establish the boundaries within which the middle ground—the everyday terrain of employee rights and denials of rights—plays out in workplaces and court cases. Measures that seem unusually severe, like punishing speech on a bumper sticker in an employee parking lot, make less extreme reactions by employers advancing their economic interests seem almost reasonable in comparison. It's hard to see how the interests of Phil Geddes and his firm were served by firing a factory worker because of a political message on her car, but there are plenty of situations where employers censor or punish employee speech because they do see strategic advantage in doing so.

Take the case of Edward Blum, who in the late 1990s was a stockbroker at Paine Webber in Houston. Blum's off-work

White House press secretary Ari Fleischer (pictured)—in referring to provocative comments made by political comedian Bill Maher after 9/11—was ridiculed for his own comments, which seemed to ignore the constitutional right to free speech.

"hobby" was political activism in opposition to affirmative action; he served in his spare time as president of a nonprofit organization devoted to this cause. In 1997 he led a campaign for a local ballot initiative that would have barred the city of Houston from hiring and contracting based on race and sex, an initiative strongly opposed by Houston's mayor at the time, Bob Lanier. Blum resigned from his job in mid-1998, charging that Paine Webber, which did a lot of bond underwriting business for the city, had pressured him to curtail his off-work political activity. Blum said a senior city official intervened with Paine Webber to try to silence him and added that the firm told him it was losing city business because of his political activities.

Mayor Lanier vehemently denied threatening Paine Webber with a loss of city contracts, but he did admit that he had complained about Blum to the firm in the run-up to the (unsuccessful) referendum on the initiative. Paine Webber, noting that Blum was not fired, said he was "asked to refrain from publishing articles with a point of view that reflected negatively on the firm's reputation and led to client complaints and a loss of business." A few months earlier, Blum had been reprimanded by Paine Webber for submitting anti–affirmative action op-ed articles to business publications. The company had a policy requiring articles written by employees to be cleared in advance, and Blum was pointedly told that "the firm will not clear for publication articles or other press contacts in which you espouse an anti–affirmative action position." (After leaving Paine Webber, Blum managed to turn his "hobby" into a career, holding positions at various conservative organizations, including most recently the American Enterprise Institute, where he spent some of his time arguing that the Voting Rights Act has outlived its usefulness.) . . .

Blum's approach to racial politics in America may appeal to some people more than others, but Paine Webber's approach to Blum comes off as an equal-opportunity affront to the very idea of free speech. Like the Alabama factory owner who fired Lynne Gobbell for her political bumper sticker, Paine Webber had a legal right to disapprove of its employees' political activities and to leverage that disapproval with terms and conditions of employment. I hasten to add here . . . that some states have laws protecting political activity by employees working for private companies, although these laws typically balance the employee's right to political speech against an employer's right to conduct business without excessive interference. Under such a law, it's hard to imagine that Gobbell wouldn't prevail, while Blum's situation seems to present more of an unpredictable collision between employee rights and employer interests.

Workplace Surveillance of the Internet

- Almost one third of companies surveyed employ dedicated staff to analyze (read) outbound e-mail

- 37% perform regular audits on outbound e-mails

- 45.5% terminated employees for violation of e-mail policies

- 26.3% said their business was impacted by the exposure of sensitive or embarrassing information

- 33.8% investigated the e-mail leak of confidential information in the past 12 months

Taken from: Martha L. Arias, "Internet Law: Workplace Surveillance of Internet Messaging Activities," Internet Business Law Services, August 6, 2007, www.ibls.com.

Freedom of speech in the workplace doesn't mean that a firm like Paine Webber has to put up with any and all employee expression on any subject at any time. Nor does it mean that an employer must allow itself to be associated with speech that contradicts its business philosophy or strategy or that departs from key principles held by its leaders. . . .

Meaningful Recourse

Situations like those that Gobbell and Blum experienced can occur without meaningful recourse for those whose speech is silenced, and without significant consequences for employers doing the silencing. A toxic combination of law, conventional economic wisdom, and accepted managerial practice has created an American workplace where freedom of speech—that most crucial of civil liberties in a healthy democracy—is something you do after work, on your own time, and even then (for many), only if your employer approves. . . . The role of law is especially important: constitutional law erects formidable potential barriers to free speech in workplaces, while employment law gives employers wide latitude to use those barriers to suppress expressive activity with impunity. The law, however, doesn't account by itself for the repressive state of free expression in the American workplace. Our legal system gives employers a great deal of discretion to manage the workplace, including employee speech, as they see fit and imposes few limits on how that discretion is exercised.

That discretion is where conventional wisdom and customary practice come in. At the risk of a bit of overgeneralization (a liberty one can take in an introduction), the civil religion that underpins work and employment in the United States is the religion of markets. In other words, we view our lives at work—the relationship between employer and worker—through a lens of property rights and contracts. The system works well, by this view, when employers are given the right of "property" ownership over not just *what* they manage but *how* they manage. Employees, in the strict market view, either accept a given employer's conditions of work or move on in the marketplace for their labor to something preferable. U.S. law . . . is more dedicated to the unbridled worship of market forces in employment, and less protective of employee rights, than the laws of other democracies with advanced economies.

But employers escape more than legal difficulties when they come down hard on employee speech; they appear just as likely to escape moral consequences. In the field of business ethics—undeniably a growth industry over the past decade—some argue that when corporations assert rights to economic autonomy in the way they do business, they incur commensurate obligations to act in moral ways toward employees and other stakeholders. In other words, a "right" to do business as you see fit doesn't operate in a moral vacuum; it comes with an obligation to respect the rights of others as moral equals, including those who work for you.

Americans may not generally agree with ethicists that rights are as important as markets. In a recent twenty-country poll of attitudes toward corporations and free markets, Americans endorsed the virtues of a free-market economy to a greater degree than respondents from all but two other countries in the poll (China and the Philippines). Americans in the poll were also less likely than those in most other countries to agree that a free market economy works best when accompanied by strong government regulation. This belief doesn't, however, translate into much confidence that employers act with moral integrity, at least as measured by attitudes toward business leaders. A Gallup poll in 2005 found only 16 percent of Americans willing to rate the honesty and ethical standards of business executives as "high" or "very high."

Limiting Free Speech

It all adds up to a kind of perfect storm for limiting free expression on or off the job. The law gives employers broad control and wide discretion. Prevailing market-focused attitudes about our economy and system of work leave employers free to be regarded as property owners who can (largely) make and enforce rules for workers as they see fit. Americans don't think highly of the moral rectitude of those who run corporations, but they aren't clamoring for more regulation to rein in the worst impulses of business leaders. So, many employers hew to a default view that even mild infringements on operational efficiency and organizational harmony are to be frowned upon and, if necessary, halted with (economic and legal) force.

Employers, then, possess not just the legal ability to repress employee speech but also all too frequently a reflexive impulse to do so. Free speech that doesn't in any serious way jeopardize the employer's interests is viewed as a potential threat, and these views are given far more weight than First Amendment rights. As an employer, I have the right to be free of even the slightest risk that your behavior will compromise my interests, even if your behavior happens to be the kind that would otherwise merit First Amendment protection.

This impulse to treat expressive behavior as threatening leads to many examples of employer overreaction, such as when DuPont fired an engineer who had sixteen years with the company for writing a book of satire about an imaginary corporation and its imaginary employees. Or when the Nationwide Insurance Company fired an employee of fifteen years who preferred not to participate in the company's effort to lobby the state legislature for a bill that went against his personal beliefs. Or when Goodwill Industries fired a sewing-machine operator because of his off-work activities as a member of the Socialist Workers Party. Or when a defense contractor in Connecticut fired a worker who declined to participate cheerfully in a Gulf War celebration. Or when the social networking firm Friendster fired a Web developer for mentioning her employer in writings posted to her personal blog.

This overreaction to what is essentially harmless employee speech on or off the job hides the effect it has on everyone else—the chill that it puts on other forms of expression by employees. . . . I will not make the indefensible claim that there is a rampant movement afoot in the American workplace to silence and punish every outbreak of non-work-related speech. I do contend, however, that a generally inhospitable workplace climate for free expression by employees puts workers on notice and at risk of consequences for their speech.

The Absence of Due Process

Limits on free speech at work go hand in hand with an absence of due-process rights and just-cause protections in the American workplace. Unlike the systems of work in most advanced nations, ours gives employers near-absolute discretion to fire employees for just about any reason, or for no reason. A person disciplined or fired for her speech enjoys no assurance of a fair process (or, for that matter, any process) for challenging that outcome. Yes, many employers elect to tolerate a wide range of speech by their workers, but there is no obligation to do so, and the lack of an inherent right to due process on the job inevitably chills employee free speech. As we will discover, workers punished for their expressive activity can in limited circumstances seek due process in the courts, but at high personal and financial cost and with little chance of success.

The natural (if frequently subconscious) apprehension that results diminishes not just our rights as employees but our effectiveness as citizens—as participants in the civic conversations that make democracy work. Work is where most adults devote significant portions of their waking lives, and where many forge the personal ties with other adults through which they construct their civic selves. Yet work in America is a place where civil liberties, including but not limited to freedom of speech, are significantly constrained, even when the exercise of those liberties poses little or no threat to the genuine interests of the employer.

What You Should Know About Censorship

Facts About Censorship in Libraries and Schools

- In 2008, 517 attempts were made to remove books from libraries and schools; in 2007, 420 attempts; and in 2006, 546 attempts.
- Since 1990, over 10,300 attempts were made to ban books from libraries and schools.
- Seventy percent of requests for book removals take place at schools; 25 percent take place at public libraries.
- Fifty-six percent of all book challenges are made by parents; 13 percent by library patrons; and 9 percent by administrators.
- Of the book challenges in 2008, 28 percent were because of explicit sexual content; 24 percent because of language; and 20 percent because of age group.
- Book challenges between 2001 and 2008 numbered 3,378:
  - 1,225 challenges due to "sexually explicit" material;
  - 1,008 challenges due to "offensive language";
  - 720 challenges due to material deemed "unsuited to age group";
  - 458 challenges due to "violence";
  - 269 challenges due to "homosexuality."
- In 2008 the most frequently banned authors included Peter Parnell and Justin Richardson, Philip Pullman, Lauren Myracle, Jim Pipe, Alvin Schwartz, Chris Crutcher, Phyllis Reynolds Naylor, Rudolfo Anaya, Stephen Chbosky, and Cecily von Ziegesar.

Facts About Censorship History in the United States

- The Sedition Act of 1798 prohibited "any false, scandalous, and malicious writing" against any branch of the U.S. government, "with the intent to defame [them], or to bring them [into] contempt or disrepute; or to excite against them [the] hatred of the good people of the United States."

- The Sedition Act of 1918 made it a crime, in wartime, "to willfully utter, print, write, or publish any disloyal, profane, scurrilous, or abusive language about the form of government of the United States, or the military or naval forces of the United States, or the flag of the United States, or the uniform of the Army or Navy of the United States."

- The Federal Communications Commission (FCC) was established by Congress in 1934 to oversee broadcast television and radio (this excludes, for example, cable television and XM radio). If the rules set by the FCC are violated by radio and television stations, the FCC can censor the station by setting fines and refusing to renew its license.

- In World War II (1941–1945), government censors previewed war correspondents' written reports from the battlefield to protect military secrets.

- The Comics Code Authority (CCA) was created in 1954 by the comic book industry to oversee comic book publications.

- The Methamphetamine Anti-Proliferation Act of 1999 outlaws the distribution of certain kinds of information detailing drug use.

- Section 215 of the Patriot Act (2001) allows government officials to review public patrons' library records.

Facts About Music Censorship

- 1951—Radio stations ban Dottie O'Brien's "Four or Five Times" and Dean Martin's "Wham Bam, Thank You Ma'am," fearing they are suggestive.

- 1954—Webb Pierce's "There Stands the Glass" is banned from radio because the lyrics are thought to condone heavy drinking.

- 1957—Producers of the *Ed Sullivan Show* instruct cameramen to show Elvis Presley only from the waist up on his third and final appearance on the program on January 7.
- 1965—Many radio stations ban the Who's single "Pictures of Lily" because the song contains a reference to masturbation.
- 1967—The Rolling Stones agree to alter the lyrics to "Let's Spend the Night Together" for an appearance on the *Ed Sullivan Show* in January. Producers request that singer Mick Jagger alter the title phrase to "Let's spend some time together."
- 1975—Because of references to birth control, radio stations refuse to play Loretta Lynn's "The Pill."
- 1985—Parents' Music Resource Center is formed by Tipper Gore and others with the stated purpose of creating a rating and advisory system for recorded music.
- 1991—Because of its depiction of domestic violence, Garth Brooks's video "The Thunder Rolls" is banned from the Nashville Network.
- 2001—The FCC fines two radio stations for playing Eminem's "The Real Slim Shady."

Facts About Book Censorship Throughout History

- 1534—Martin Luther's translation of the Bible is considered heretical, and copies are burned.
- 1559—The List of Forbidden Books is established by the Catholic Church under Pope Paul VI. In 1948 the list included four thousand books; in 1966, the list was abolished.
- 1650—A publication by William Pynchon is burned in the market square in Boston.
- 1792—Thomas Paine is indicted for treason in England because *The Rights of Man* defended the French Revolution.
- 1873—The Comstock Law is established in the United States. Classic literature, including the *Canterbury Tales* and *Moll Flanders*, are banned from shipment through the U.S. mail. The Comstock Law would also forbid birth control information from being distributed through the mail, leading to the arrest of Margaret Sanger in 1915.

- 1929—The Tarzan books, written by Edgar Rice Burroughs, are banned in Los Angeles because Tarzan and Jane live together but are unmarried.
- 1933—On May 10, at the bequest of the German Student Association, twenty-five thousand "un-German" books are burned in Nazi Germany.
- 1957—U.S. Customs officials seize copies of Allen Ginsberg's "Howl," believing the poem to be obscene. A state court ruled that local authorities could not suppress the distribution of the poem.
- 1989—"Little Red Riding Hood" is banned in two school districts in California because illustrations pictured the character carrying wine to her grandmother.
- 1990s—Libraries containing Albanian language collections are burned in Kosovo.
- 1990–2004—The American Library Association lists the top ten banned authors over the past fifteen years: Alvin Schwartz, Judy Blume, Robert Cormier, J.K. Rowling, Michael Willhoite, Katherine Paterson, Stephen King, Maya Angelou, R.L. Stine, and John Steinbeck.

Facts About Movie Censorship

- 1909—The New York Board of Motion Picture Censors is founded.
- 1915—*The Birth of a Nation*, an adaptation of Thomas Dixon's *The Clansman*, is banned in Chicago, Kansas City, and Philadelphia, due to racist themes.
- 1930—The Motion Picture Production Code is founded. In 1934 the Production Code Administration (PCA) begins to oversee movies released in the United States. The organization will operate until 1968.
- 1930—*All Quiet on the Western Front* is banned in Germany and Italy.
- 1943–46—the Production Code Administration (PCA) requests changes for Howard Hughes's *The Outlaw*; in 1946, Hughes releases the movie without the PCA's approval.

- 1961—Luis Buñuel's *Viridiana* is banned in Spain.
- 1974—*The Texas Chainsaw Massacre* is banned in Finland, Britain, Australia, West Germany, Chile, Iceland, Ireland, Norway, Sweden, and Singapore.
- 1988—Several southern cities in the United States ban Martin Scorsese's adaptation of *The Last Temptation of Christ*.
- 2007—Will Smith's *I Am Legend* is banned in China.

What You Should Do About Censorship

Censorship has been a divisive issue even in countries like the United States, where free speech is protected by the Constitution. Questions such as what should be censored and who should oversee the censorship have been answered in a variety of ways at different times in different cultures. Censorship has been practiced by religious organizations, governments, the media, and private corporations for a variety of reasons.

Free speech advocates like the American Civil Liberties Union (ACLU) have argued against all forms of censorship, believing that individuals should have free access to any information they wish to view. These views have clashed with organizations like Enough Is Enough that argue that children should be protected from certain kinds of information on the Internet, such as pornography. Still other organizations, including the military and police forces of many countries, have maintained that censorship is sometimes necessary to protect important secrets.

Learn More About the Issue

In order to form an opinion, debate, and take action on the issue of censorship, it is important to know more about both the history of the issue and the parameters of the current debate. You might begin by gathering information about censorship in both your own and other countries. How has censorship changed through history? How has new technology (like the Internet) impacted censorship? How does one country's method of censorship differ from that of another's? How does censorship change during times of war? It may also be helpful to research primary documents such as the constitution of your country along with information about court cases focusing on the issue of censorship.

Much of this information can be found in your school and public libraries. Encyclopedias and dictionaries are frequently a good source of basic information, while more narrowly focused books will address specific court cases and historic instances of censorship. Periodicals and newspapers offer a more immediate, or "ground level," view of how people react and have reacted to censorship issues in their own time. Teachers and librarians can also suggest how to access resources specific to your school, such as the school board's written policy about books and other materials that are used in the classroom.

Define the Debate

As with any contentious issue, the censorship debate has many sides, and understanding these various positions will help define the parameters of that debate. Organizations representing different viewpoints frequently have pamphlets and other materials outlining their positions. Most organizations also have Internet sites, allowing easy access to an organization's current activities and even providing links to similar sites.

As you gather information from various sites, what recurring ideas appear within the broader issue of censorship? Do certain organizations focus on a limited set of ideas within the debate or approach the issue of censorship more generally? Are the ideas that each organization focuses on related to contemporary controversies, or do these ideas relate to long-running questions within the censorship debate? Other information, such as surveys from various polling organizations, can help clarify how the broader public views the issue of censorship.

Finally, you can learn more about the issue by attending a meeting of the local school board that addresses the issue of censorship, such as the banning of a book from a classroom. What are the opinions of the teachers, parents, and students involved? How are these arguments similar to or different than the arguments presented by censorship organizations?

Form an Opinion

Ultimately, learning more about and defining the debate on censorship offers the groundwork needed to begin forming your own opinion. As you read various viewpoints about censorship, perhaps you agreed with some, disagreed with others, and remained undecided about others. It is possible that you will find an organization whose views you share, but it is just as likely that you will find plausible points in multiple organizations. As you weigh the various arguments, you might also question how your opinions have been formed. Are they the same as your parents or guardians or teachers? Have they changed on specific censorship issues over time or remained the same? Have your opinions been formed by secondary observation or actual experience?

Many arguments—both pro and con—may also seem abstract unless you have lived through them. One method of forming an opinion would be to ask yourself how you would think or feel in a particular situation. For instance, how would you feel if you wrote an article for the school newspaper, but the school administration refused to publish it? Would you feel that your rights had been violated? Or would you agree that schools have the right to censor material they consider controversial?

You might also consider an example from your own experience. For instance, many school and public libraries use filtering technology to protect children and teenagers from pornography and other potentially harmful material on the Internet. Is this a form of censorship or simply a common sense way of protecting underage children?

Take Action

Forming an opinion on an issue of censorship may also inspire you to take action. This might include writing a letter to the editor of the local newspaper or perhaps writing a letter to your school board about a particular censorship policy. Many people get involved with issues by joining an organization, and many organizations sponsor activities ranging from contacting government officials (legislators, Congresspersons) to public rallies. Other possibilities include forming your own organization with like-minded friends and starting a blog on the Internet. Finally, many people serve as interns at an organization like the ACLU or Enough Is

Enough, or even become involved in an appeal or a challenge at their local school board.

Whether you decide to take action or not on the issue of censorship, your research and background information will help you to make informed decisions about the debate. You will not only understand the history and parameters of the censorship argument but also will be capable of adding valuable input and explaining your own position on the issue.

ORGANIZATIONS TO CONTACT

American Civil Liberties Union (ACLU)
125 Broad St., 18th Fl., New York, NY 10004
(212) 549-2500
e-mail: aclu@aclu.org
Web site: www.aclu.org

The ACLU is a national organization that defends Americans' civil rights as guaranteed in the U.S. Constitution. It advocates for freedom of all forms of speech, including pornography, flag-burning, and political protest. The ACLU offers numerous reports, fact sheets, and policy statements on free speech issues, which are freely available on its Web site. Some of these publications include "Free Speech Under Fire," "Freedom of Expression," and, for students, "Ask Sybil Liberty About Your Right to Free Expression."

American Library Association (ALA)
50 E. Huron St., Chicago, IL 60611
(800) 545-2433
e-mail: ala@ala.org
Web site: www.ala.org

The ALA is the primary professional organization for librarians in the United States. Through its Office for Intellectual Freedom (OIF), the ALA supports free access to libraries and library materials. The OIF also monitors and opposes efforts to ban books from libraries. Its publications, which are freely available on its Web site, include "Intellectual Freedom and Censorship Q & A," the "Library Bill of Rights," and the "Freedom to Read Statement."

Canadian Association for Free Expression (CAFE)
PO Box 332, Station 'B,' Etobicoke, ON M9W 5L3, Canada
(905) 277-3914
e-mail: cafe@canadafirst.net
Web site: www.canadianfreespeech.com

CAFE, one of Canada's leading civil liberties groups, works to strengthen the freedom of speech and freedom of expression provisions in the Canadian Charter of Rights and Freedoms. It lobbies politicians and researches threats to freedom of speech. Publications include specialized reports, leaflets, and *The Free Speech Monitor*, which is published ten times per year.

Concerned Women for America (CWA)

1015 Fifteenth St. NW, Ste. 1100, Washington, DC 20005
(202) 488-7000
Web site: www.cwfa.org

CWA is a membership organization that promotes Christian values and works to create a society that is conducive to forming families and raising healthy children. Opposition to pornography is one of CWA's six major focuses. Its publications include the monthly *Family Voice* magazine, which has addressed such topics as "Filters in Libraries: Protecting Our Kids."

Electronic Frontier Foundation (EFF)

454 Shotwell St., San Francisco, CA 94110-1914
(415) 436-9333
e-mail: information@eff.org
Web site: www.eff.org

EFF is a nonprofit, nonpartisan organization that works to protect privacy, freedom of speech, and other rights in the digital world. Fighting censorship on the Internet is one of its core missions. Its publications, which are freely available on its Web site, include a "Legal Guide for Bloggers" and white papers such as "Noncommercial Email Lists: Collateral Damage in the Fight Against Spam."

Family Research Council (FRC)

801 G St. NW, Washington, DC 20001
(800) 225-4008
Web site: www.frc.org

The FRC is a faith-based organization that seeks to promote marriage and family. It believes that pornography harms women, children, and families, and therefore the FRC seeks to strengthen current obscenity laws. It publishes a variety of books, policy papers, fact sheets, and other materials, including the brochure *Dealing with Pornography: A Practical Guide for Protecting Your Family and Your Community* and the book *Protecting Your Child in an X-Rated World: What You Need to Know to Make a Difference*.

Federal Communications Commission (FCC)
445 Twelfth St. SW, Washington, DC 20554
(888) 225-5322
e-mail: fccinfo@fcc.gov
Web site: www.fcc.gov

The FCC is an independent government agency responsible for regulating telecommunications. Among other duties, it enforces federal laws related to broadcast indecency. The FCC publishes various reports, updates, and reviews that can be accessed online at its Web site.

Foundation for Individual Rights in Education (FIRE)
601 Walnut St., Ste. 510, Philadelphia, PA 19106
(215) 717-3473
e-mail: fire@thefire.org
Web site: www.thefire.org

FIRE was founded in 1999 to defend the rights of students and professors at American colleges and universities. The group advocates for and provides legal assistance to students and professors who feel that their individual rights, particularly their right to free speech, have been violated. Its publications include *FIRE's Guide to Free Speech on Campus* and "Spotlight: The Campus Freedom Resource," which contains information about speech codes at specific colleges and universities.

Free Expression Policy Project (FEPP)
170 West 76 St., Ste. 301, New York, NY 10023
e-mail: margeheins@verizon.net
Web site: www.fepproject.org

FEPP is a project of the Democracy Program at New York University School of Law's Brennan Center for Justice. FEPP promotes freedom of expression, but in a "non-absolutist" fashion; it believes that certain forms of speech, such as harassing and threatening speech, are not entitled to First Amendment protection. Its publications include fact sheets, commentaries, and policy reports, which are freely available on its Web site.

Free Speech Coalition
PO Box 10480, Canoga Park, CA 91309
(818) 348-9373
Web site: www.freespeechcoalition.com

The coalition is a trade association that represents members of the adult entertainment industry. It seeks to protect the industry from attempts to censor pornography. Its publications include the journal *Free Speaker* and the weekly *Free Speech X-Press*.

Freedom Forum
555 Pennsylvania Ave. NW, Washington, DC 20001
(202) 292-6100
e-mail: news@freedomforum.org
Web site: www.freedomforum.org

The Freedom Forum was founded in 1991 to defend a free press and free speech. It operates the Newseum (a museum of news and the news media) and the First Amendment Center, which works to educate the public about free speech and other First Amendment issues. Its publications include an annual *State of the First Amendment* survey, and the First Amendment Center maintains on its Web site a First Amendment Library that serves as a clearinghouse for judicial, legislative, and other material on First Amendment freedoms.

International Freedom of Expression Exchange (IFEX)
The IFEX Clearing House
555 Richmond St. West, Ste. 1101, PO Box 407, Toronto, ON
M5V 3B1, Canada
(416) 515-9622
e-mail: ifex@ifex.org
Web site: www.ifex.org

IFEX consists of more than forty organizations that support the freedom of expression. Its work is coordinated by the Toronto-based Clearing House. Through the Action Alert Network, organizations report abuses of free expression to the Clearing House, which distributes that information throughout the world. Publications include the weekly *Communiqué*, which reports on free expression triumphs and violations.

Morality in Media (MIM)
475 Riverside Dr., Ste. 239, New York, NY 10115
(212) 870-3222
e-mail: mim@moralityinmedia.org
Web site: www.moralityinmedia.org

MIM is a national interfaith organization that fights obscenity and indecency in the media. It works to educate the public on obscenity issues and maintains the National Obscenity Law Center, a clearinghouse of legal materials on obscenity law. Its publications include the reports *Stranger in the House*, *Pornography's Effects on Adults and Children*, and the bimonthly *Morality in Media Newsletter*.

National Coalition Against Censorship (NCAC)
275 Seventh Ave., Ste. 1504, New York, NY 10001
(212) 807-6222
e-mail: ncac@ncac.org
Web site: www.ncac.org

The NCAC is an alliance of national not-for-profit organizations, including literary, artistic, religious, educational, professional, labor, and civil liberties groups. The coalition works to defend freedom of thought, inquiry, and expression and to fight censorship. Its Web site provides access to press releases, legal briefs, and congressional testimony on censorship issues.

National Coalition for the Protection of Children and Families
800 Compton Rd., Ste. 9224, Cincinnati, OH 45231
(513) 521-6227

e-mail: ncpcf@nationalcoalition.org
Web site: www.nationalcoalition.org

The coalition is a Christian organization that encourages traditional sexual ethics and fights pornography. It encourages strong regulation of adult bookstores and the use of Internet filters in public libraries. Its publications include the *Library Protection Plan* and the booklet *Pornography: The Deconstruction of Human Sexuality.*

People for the American Way (PFAW)
2000 M St. NW, Ste. 400, Washington, DC 20036
(202) 467-4999 or 1-800-326-PFAW
e-mail: pfaw@pfaw.org
Web site: www.pfaw.org

PFAW works to promote citizen participation in democracy and safeguard the principles of the U.S. Constitution, including the right to free speech. It publishes a variety of fact sheets, articles, and position statements on its Web site and distributes the e-mail newsletter *Freedom to Learn Online.*

Rutherford Institute
PO Box 7482, Charlottesville, VA 22906-7482
(434) 978-3888
e-mail: staff@rutherford.org
Web site: www.rutherford.org

The Rutherford Institute is a conservative organization that was founded to defend First Amendment rights, including the right to freedom of speech and freedom of religion. The institute provides free legal aid to people who believe that their rights to these freedoms have been violated. The Rutherford Institute's publications, which are freely available on its Web site, include "Through the Looking Glass: What Are Young People Learning from Unconstitutional Religious Censorship?" and "Zero Tolerance for God? Religious Expression in the Workplace."

BIBLIOGRAPHY

Books

Peter Blecha, *Taboo Tunes: A History of Banned Bands and Censored Songs*. New York: Backbeat, 2004.

Cathy Byrd and Susan Richmond, eds. *Potentially Harmful: The Art of American Censorship*. Atlanta: Georgia State University, 2006.

J.M. Coetzee, *Giving Offence: Essays on Censorship*. Chicago: University of Chicago Press, 1997.

Francis G. Couvares, ed., *Movie Censorship and American Culture*. Amherst, MA: University of Massachusetts Press, 2006.

Jonathan Dollimore, *Sex, Literature and Censorship*. Cambridge, UK: Polity, 2001.

Leonard Freedman, *The Offensive Art: Political Satire and Its Censorship Around the World from Beerbohm to Borat*. Santa Barbara, CA: Praeger, 2008.

Marjorie Heins, *Not in Front of the Children: "Indecency," Censorship, and the Innocence of Youth*. Chapel Hill, NC: Rutgers University Press, 2007.

———, *Sex, Sin, and Blasphemy: A Guide to America's Censorship Wars*. New York: New Press, 1993.

John H. Houchin, *Censorship of the American Theatre in the Twentieth Century*. New York: Cambridge University Press, 2009.

Brian Jennings, *Censorship: The Threat to Silence Talk Radio*. New York: Threshold Editions, 2009.

Nicholas J. Karolides, Margaret Bald, and Dawn B. Sova, *120 Banned Books: Censorship Histories of World Literature*. New York: Checkmark, 2005.

John R. MacArthur, *Second Front: Censorship and Propaganda in the 1991 Gulf War*. Berkeley: University of California Press, 2004.

Eric Nuzum, *Parental Advisory: Music Censorship in America*. New York: Harper, 2001.

Brad O'Leary, *Shut Up, America! The End of Free Speech*. Washington, DC: WND, 2009.

Lawrence Soley, *Censorship, Inc: The Corporate Threat to Free Speech in the United States*. New York: Monthly Review, 2002.

Periodicals

Advocate, "Battling the Military Ban," March 2009.

American Libraries, "Politics Heats Up Materials Challenges," June/July 2009.

Economist, "Damned if You Do; China's Internet Censors," June 27, 2009.

Theresa Gilbert, "Banning Pro-Life on Campus: Capilano, Guelph, and McGill," *Catholic Insight*, January 2009.

Michelle Greppi, "A High- to Low-Brow Night," *Television Week*, December 1, 2008.

Ezra Levant, "The Internet Saved My Tongue: How I Beat Canada's 'Human Rights' Censors," *Reason*, June 2009.

Brian Lowry, "The SPAM Filter Promotes Pundit Accountability," *Variety*, April 6, 2009.

Douglas MacMillan, "Google, Yahoo Criticized Over Foreign Censorship," BusinessWeek Online, March 16, 2009.

Evgeny Morozov, "To Stop Dissent, Call It Smut," *Newsweek International*, February 2, 2009.

————, "Do-It-Yourself Censorship," *Newsweek International*, March 16, 2009.

————, "Control Issues," *Newsweek International*, June 29, 2009.

PC Magazine Online, "Iraq Weighs Internet Censorship," August 5, 2009.

Progressive, "A Literary Bust in Jerusalem," July 2009.

Jeffrey Rosen, "Freespeeech on the Web: Is the Internet Really the Bastion of Free Expression That We Think It Is?" *New York Times Upfront*, January 12, 2009.

Nick Summers, "Keeping Facebook Nice and Clean," *Newsweek International*, June 1, 2009.

David Talbot, "Dissent Made Safer: How Anonymity Technology Could Save Free Speech on the Internet," *Technology Review*, May/June 2009.

W, "Un Censored," November 2008.

Christopher Werth, "The Censors Right Here at Home," *Newsweek International*, May 25, 2009.

Debra Lau Whelan, "A Dirty Little Secret: Self-Censorship Is Rampant and Lethal," *School Library Journal*, February 2009.

INDEX

PICTURE CREDITS

Maury Aaseng, 13, 19, 26, 33, 51, 57, 76, 86, 95
AP Images, 31, 37, 44, 48, 55, 70, 77,
© Caro/Alamy, 6
Larry Downing/Reuters/Landov, 93
Getty Images, 83
Fred Prouser/Reuters/Landov, 65
© Jim Sulley/epa/Corbis, 28
Kwame Zikomo/SuperStock, 11, 17